First published by AuthorHouse   16/05/2011, under the ISBNs

978-1-4567-8013-5(sc),

978-1-4567-8012-8(e).

3rd Edition Published by CreateSpace 6/1/14 – ISBNs

978-1494927332

1494927330

I am fundraising in support of Help for Heroes; with the aim to raise at least
£1,000. Help For Heroes do fantastic work supporting our service personnel
and their families and I am sure that they would be extremely grateful for
any help or donation that you can give. Please go to my fundraising page to
see what I have donated already: www.bmycharity.com/lshapedvillage.

The L-Shaped Village

Book One: **Art and the Artisans**

By

LEE J. H. FOMES

<u>Acknowledgements</u>

I must thank a number of people who unwittingly made a huge difference to my general confidence in life, and who showed their unwavering support, without which this book would not be in your hands:

A *huge* thank you to my wife Hannah, who made my school and college days more memorable, and for her unwavering support when things weren't so good for me; to my twins William and Molly, who make me laugh harder than anyone; to my parents for all their support in everything I have tried to do; to my sister Claudia, who brought the essence of the Village to life on canvas; to my editor Sarah Cheeseman, whose incredible patience with my manuscript and unbelievable attention to detail taught me so much; to Colin Anderson for believing in me when few did, and to Ed Keeley for believing *him*; to Craig Philbin for everything he has done for me; and lastly but SO not least, to Colin Tooke, whose perfect example of friendship makes me wish I'd known him all my life.

For Hannah, Molly and William.

Prologue

December 2006

Tradition was what had led Art to this point. Making new traditions, an ironic statement in itself, had been the main reason he stood facing the main entrance to St David's Hospital on the same crisp, cold December night every year, with a large bag slung over his shoulder. It had not always been as large, but Art could no longer remember it being any smaller than it was now. The years he had been doing this had merged into what seemed like a month of these evenings, and the familiarity of the cold and the darkness was both welcoming and comforting.

He moved to the side of the entrance so that he could still see who was coming out, but had enough time to dart out of sight if it wasn't her. He waited, watching his breath forming clouds as he exhaled. *She should be here any time now*, he thought. That was the arrangement – she would come and meet him at the main entrance, and they would discuss how he could do what he was here to do without anyone knowing he had ever been there. Every year, without fail.

There was movement from inside the hospital – two figures emerged, moving swiftly. Art darted behind the wall of the tunnel-like entrance quietly and waited for them to disappear. They burst through the doors – two women dressed in nurses' uniforms with thick coats over the top and red tinsel in their hair. They walked swiftly, arm in arm, chatting happily as they headed for one of the cars in the staff car park. Art listened to their cheerful conversation as it died away to nothing and their figures became little more than moving dots in the distance.

Art moved back around the wall and into sight of the entrance. He suddenly came face-to-face with a tall woman in a white coat and a stethoscope around her neck.

'Boo!' she shouted.

Art jumped out of his skin. 'Whoa, Dr Levvy! How did you…'

'A regular Ninja Warrior, me,' she whispered, smiling. She gave him a quick hug and then motioned for him to follow her.

Art looked left and right, over his shoulder and then followed. They walked into the hospital, past the car parking meters and the reception desk, and into a small side office that was dark and obviously empty. Dawn Levvy switched on the light when Art had wrestled his bag through the doorframe and closed the door. She pulled down the blind and twisted the lock. Art carefully placed the bag down on the floor by his feet and pulled out a chair from under the table for himself. Dawn sat down beside him and turned to face him.

'So here we are again, young man,' she said.

Art smiled at her. 'I knew you'd come,' he said.

'Of course I did. I got your note, as usual. I like your style this year – expensive paper. Embossed envelope, too.'

Art looked puzzled. 'But I didn't send you a note this year – I just figured you'd remember.'

Dawn gave him a sly smile. 'I'd know your handwriting anywhere by now,' she said; 'you really went all out this year.'

Art thought hard, but was sure he had not bothered with the usual note. How could he have been wrong about that? He was sure he wasn't. But before he could protest any further, Dawn pulled her chair closer and dropped her voice.

'It should be easy this year,' she said; 'there's hardly anyone on the wards and there's less staff on, so you should have no trouble. The only problem I can see is actually placing it near the children's beds. There are a few beds empty, and that means the nurses will be able to keep a closer eye on everyone, which means bad news for you.'

'Is the lift working?' Art asked.

'Yes, but I'd steer clear of it. You can hear the floor announcements from the lift well before it arrives: you'll give yourself away. Here's the plan.'

Art stood in the quiet pitch-black corridor with his nose pressed up against the window, looking out across the courtyard at the next building. Only a few of the lights were on in the whole of the block, all twenty storeys. *Any second now...* he thought. And sure enough, one of the rooms on the third floor illuminated, then went dark, then illuminated again. *There's the signal*, he thought. Art knew the main corridor would be clear now, and he sprinted towards it with a feeling of excitement rushing through him. He found the main corridor brightly lit and totally deserted as he ran down it, being careful not to knock the bag he was carrying. He reached the stairwell doors, pressed his way through them and began the four-storey climb.

At the doors to the fourth floor, Art checked his watch: maybe ten minutes left – this was going to be close. No more than usual though, and this was how he liked it. He slowly pushed open one of the big double doors and poked his head through. There was a large deserted reception area lit with fluorescent lighting, and coffee machines were lined up along one wall. To the left was a corridor leading to a tunnel bridge that linked the two buildings together. There was no one in sight, so Art dragged himself through the doors and ran for the corridor. At the far end, he found himself in a newly refurbished area of the hospital; it was a large café with a row of offices on the left-hand side. He headed for the third one and darted inside. Closing the door behind him, he flicked on the lights, turned them off again, then on once more. He hoped that Dr Levvy had seen the return signal.

Giving her time to navigate through the building to the next checkpoint, Art checked his watch again; just five minutes left now. He pressed his face to the window and looked out at the building he had just come from. *Any*

7

second... he thought. Another minute was all he could spare at this checkpoint – she was going to have to be quick. His watch ticked closer and closer towards the deadline. *Any second...* Four minutes. *Where is she?* Three and a half minutes. *Come on, come on – where's the signal?* Three minutes. Art thought hard. Never had he missed a deadline in all these long years, and the last push towards the final stairwell was at least two minutes hard running. This was getting way too close. He held on for another fifteen seconds, then decided it was time to act. He would just have to hope that the corridor leading behind the X-Ray Department was clear.

He slung the huge bag over his shoulder and opened the door slowly, poking his head through to check the coast was still clear. The café looked exactly the same, except that one of the fluorescent lights was flickering slightly, as if it had just come on again. Art dismissed this and slipped through the door, clicking it shut quietly behind him. He headed to the far end of the café where huge illuminated signs pointed the way to the X-Ray Department, and began the last phase of the logistics plan that would get him to his goal.

The corridor was almost a hundred metres long, with several square archways along the left wall leading off to various sections within the department. One more left turn at the end of the corridor, and a few yards in front of him would be the final stairwell. He ran as fast as he could without shaking the bag, adrenaline pumping through him as he neared the last corner. He rushed past a cleaner's trolley without paying attention, his mind fixed on getting to the stairwell, and slipped on a patch of wet floor. His left leg flew out in front of him, but his momentum was enough to stop him falling straight away. He had time to swing the bag round, cradle it in his arms and turn to his left before he fell to the floor and slammed into the far wall. The sound was ear-splitting, and to his horror he saw that the stairwell doors were blocked with lots of people. That's why there had been no signal; he should have allowed more time. He stayed as still as he could, but was helpless to do anything as they all began to turn their heads as one. Art shut his eyes, sure that his secret was out. After all these years of anonymity, this was the year he would have to come clean. He could only imagine the taunting he would get at school for this, the confused look his parents would give him and the feeling of sheer embarrassment when people found out. He opened his eyes slowly and sighed, resigned to the fact that he would be explaining this for the next few minutes at least before he could get going again and reluctantly finish his task. He would finish, of that he was sure. This would not stop him.

As he cowered on the hard floor awaiting the inevitable, he felt a very slight vibration beneath him. An extremely low humming sound seemed to permeate through everything around him, which slowed down and eventually ground to a halt. He looked around, wondering what had happened, and stared at the crowd standing in front of the stairs. All the figures around the poorly lit stairwell were all standing stock still – like statues in the dark – and had turned their heads towards him, but hadn't quite made eye contact. It was as if they had been paused halfway through the movement. Art slowly got to his feet, transfixed by the sight, and without thinking he left the bag on the floor and crept closer to the figures. There was complete silence, like standing in a soundproofed studio, closed off from any noise that could ever be made. He stood just a few feet away now, totally confused as to what was happening.

And then he saw it: movement from the back of the crowd. A small figure in comparison to the rest, only slightly smaller than himself, shrouded in darkness, was walking through them towards him. Art's pulse was racing, but now out of fear and confusion, all his excitement gone.

The figure came closer and closer, making only a slight noise as his feet squashed into the floor. He passed through the crowd and Art could begin to make out his features. He was smiling ever so slightly with kind but keen eyes of piercing blue; a roundish face with a black beret pressed down to one side, his hands hanging to his sides, and a sleek but strong-looking frame. Even though he was just under Art's height, he looked like an adult, no hint

9

of youth in his eyes or any of his other features. He was wearing a black raincoat, tight black trousers and very small but compact boots laced halfway up to his knees. He stopped just a foot or two from Art and smiled wider still.

'W…who are you?' Art stammered.

The little man smiled, then laughed loudly.

'The question that answers everything, and it's the first thing I hear from your lips. No further proof needed. Hello, Art,' he replied.

Art's eyes widened when he heard his own name.

'How do you know me?'

The man laughed again.

'That's really it? That's all you're going to ask me? Not w*hat's happened to all these people*, or *what was that bizarre noise I heard just now?* Well I'll tell you. You'll believe me, 'cos you can see it with your own eyes. That lot,' he pointed back to the crowd of people with his thumb, 'are encapsulated in a small time pocket, so they look frozen to you but are actually just moving very slowly. If Pud and Jimma are right – if they can ever stop arguing – it should be roughly one minute for them for every second of ours. And that excruciating humming was the sound of space-time being forced to give up some of its laws, so that no one finds you out *and* so that we can have this little chat.' He folded his arms, looking very pleased with himself.

Art looked at the people, and sure enough some of them looked like they had turned their heads a little further in the time they had been speaking.

'Yes, that's right, Slippy-Over-Boy, they'll be looking right this way quite soon. I suggest we scarper, pronto!' And he began to wind his way back through the crowd. 'Come on, then; stop gawping and let's get out of here, shall we?'

Art could not understand what was happening or who this mysterious little man was, but his instinct was to follow him, although he had no idea why. He ran back for his bag, slung it over his shoulder and headed around

10

the outside of the crowd. The little man had disappeared into a small office and was holding the door open for Art. He followed, and found himself once again sat at a large desk, but this time facing the small man who had just saved him from being found out. The man closed the door and pulled out a little bottle with a cork in the top from inside his coat. He uncorked it, pulled out a little dropper, drew up some rather oddly coloured liquid and allowed a single drop to fall to the floor. As it hit the carpet, another low humming sound went right through Art's head, like having his ears syringed, and movement resumed on the other side of the frosted glass door.

The man sat down in a rather large chair that made him look even smaller and started to unpack the contents of a small backpack that had been rather neatly concealed behind his back. He got out a rather battered but shining metal tankard and two little screw-top bottles, one filled with black powder, the other a sort of light brown. He poured a little of each into his tankard, then pulled a gourd of water from his backpack and filled the tankard up to the top. Then he reached into his inside pocket and pulled out another little stopper-bottle, this time filling it with perfectly clear but vigorously bubbling liquid. He let one drop fall into his tankard, which immediately started bubbling and steaming like it was boiling. He pulled out what looked like a miniature oar made of silver and started stirring as he looked up at Art.

'My name is Maga. I come from a faraway place that you can get to in an instant if you know the right people. Fortunately for me, I do,' he said. He stopped stirring and took a sip from his tankard.

'You mean Pud and Jimma?' Art asked.

Maga raised his eyebrows. 'Oooh, you picked that up even under stress? I'm impressed. Not bad for a human,' he replied. 'I'm beginning to understand why the Boss is so interested in you.'

Art could see Maga's face clearly now and was struck by how piercing his eyes were. The only way Art could think of describing the way they made him look was 'fiercely intelligent', but at the same time there was an unmistakable air of childish mischief around the eyes and mouth. This little person looked like a man, but unlike any Art had ever seen. The more he looked at Maga, the more he thought about what he had just said – *not bad for a human.*

'You ... aren't human?' he managed to utter.

Maga laughed, put his tankard down and sprang out of his seat. He started doing backflips across the table and running along on his hands. He flipped over and landed lightly on his feet, pulled out a set of juggling balls and started doing impossibly fast cascades, bouncing them off every part of his body; then in an instant they were out of sight and he was back in his seat again, sipping from his tankard.

'You could say that,' he said. 'I suppose you could call me a *sprite.*'

Art looked confused. 'Well, you sort of look human,' he said, 'just a bit smaller.'

Art looked for the telltale signs that might give him away as a fairy or any other fictional type of humanoid he had read or heard about – Maga's ears looked perfectly normal, as did his nose, and even though his beret was slightly odd, it still wasn't outside the realms of normality; in fact, it looked almost military.

'Put it this way,' Maga said, 'I'm no older than you are, but I've been around for *hundreds* of years. I've never grown up, but I've seen *everything*, in *every* time and *every* place. Just imagine all those years of experience and knowledge, in the head of a *child*, and you might come close.'

He leaned forward in his chair and tapped the side of his head.

'I could show you things in here that would curdle your custard,' he continued, 'and someday I'll grow old enough to appreciate them, or so I'm told. Until then, they just make me incredibly intelligent, more experienced than anyone you'll ever meet, and one of the best field agents there's ever been.'

He sat back and folded his arms. He sounded like a child announcing that he was the oldest in the room and the most important.

12

'A field agent? Who for?' asked Art.

'Ha! You're not getting it out of me that easily! The Boss said you'd be a wily one. Now forget all of that – time's ticking on, remember?'

Art's eyes widened; he had forgotten all about his deadline. He flashed his watch in front of his eyes: less than fifteen seconds left. This year he would fail. This year he would not be there before midnight and all the mystery would be lost. He rushed to the window where he could see the lights flashing on and off frantically in a room halfway up the building opposite. The coast had obviously been clear for a while, and Dr Levvy was clearly worried he had not seen the signal, having not given her the final double flash from the top floor to say he was there, on time, and on his way back. There would be no chance now. He would still complete the mission, but his clean record would be broken. He slumped down into the nearest chair and closed his eyes in defeat. Just as he began to wonder if there was *some* way he could salvage the situation, a low hum vibrated through his head and the air around him seemed to come to a standstill. He looked up to see Maga with the little dropper in his hand, holding it out over the floor.

'When you've quite finished wallowing in self-pity we have a job to do, and less than five seconds left to do it in. Well, I say five seconds…'

Chapter One

Children's Ward

Four years later, December 2010

With midnight in less than ten minutes' time, Charge Nurse Jenny Hopkins was beginning to think he had forgotten. Not in the five years she had been there had he forgotten. Sure, it was a lot to expect, but the difference it made to the children was immeasurable. And it was nearly Christmas Day, after all.

To the children, though, it was still firmly Christmas Eve. Almost two hours ago, the last of them – the little girl with the red hair – had given up her struggle to stay awake to finally see Santa at work, and drifted off to sleep.

Jenny checked on each of the children in turn, throwing a sly look at her watch every ten minutes or so, then returned to her position behind the desk in the main reception area. She reached into the large tin containing the mince pies brought in by the SHO, took out a particularly small one and bit into it.

Just then, the others finished their rounds of Caterpillar Ward and Ladybird Ward and leaned over the desk with sarcastic looks on their faces.

'Looks like he's not coming, doesn't it?' said James, the tall and rather famously lanky staff nurse, known for his tact and sensitive side. 'I knew the rumours weren't true. I mean, what kind of person dumps a load of unwanted toys in a hospital in the middle of the night and then runs for it? If you ask me, I'm glad he didn't show – it means there's one less nutter in the

14

world than I thought.' He reached into the tin and took an overly large mince pie.

Jenny was always offended by his cavalier attitude, and stood up to reprimand him yet again.

'For your information there is ten minutes to go before midnight, so he or she may still make it.' She threw her half-finished mince pie into the bin angrily. 'And another thing,' she continued, 'they are not unwanted toys. They're made especially for the kids, and they love them.'

James relaxed his stance even further, retaining his smug expression. It was almost too much for Jenny to bear.

'Oh, I don't know why I'm explaining myself to you,' she said, 'you'll see soon enough,' and she stormed off to check on the kids again, just to get away from his arrogance.

Underneath it all, though, she was starting to feel a little disappointed. This time last year, they were already staring at the large sack that had somehow appeared in the middle of the floor, ready to be sorted into piles of two or three for each child, depending on how full the ward was. She was the only remaining member of staff at the Children's Ward from the previous year, and was the only one who remembered the look on the children's faces as they woke up and saw the pile of presents at their feet.

Jenny was thinking of the little boy with the broken hand several years earlier who couldn't open any of his presents, and how she had sat with him and opened them for him. Like all the children that year, he was way too excited by the sight of all the colourful presents to feel in the slightest bit sorry for himself, and quite forgot he was injured at all. Jenny had been perhaps the most thankful for them that year.

She was just starting to resign herself to the fact that maybe he had forgotten when the telephone rang, which struck her as very odd, as the telephone rarely rang in the dark hours. Operations rarely took place during the night-time either, and the last of the medication had been administered hours ago. Jenny quickly ran back to answer it.

'Hello, Children's Ward,' she said brightly.

The voice on the other end sounded distinctly feminine.

'Hello, err...' it coughed and cleared its throat, then said again in a deeper voice, 'Err, hello, Nurse Hopkins.'

Jenny could not remember saying her name when she picked up the phone. The voice went on.

'This is Doctor Phillips here. I wonder if you could gather all your staff together for a general briefing. You see, we on the Board are rather worried about security this year, what with the recent spate of local robberies. We're counting on you down-to-earth nursing chappies to keep us all safe and well this festive season, and, well that's pretty much it. Gather all your staff together and make them aware, would you? Oh, and err, Merry Christmas.'

The line went dead.

Jenny wondered why she hadn't heard of the robberies in the area, and why Dr Phillips had sounded so feminine to start with. And why, indeed, he was phoning around the wards at such an obscene time of night. He had been his usual arrogant self, however, no change there, so with a shrug she put down the receiver and gathered everyone together for the briefing.

They all displayed similar expressions of bafflement when she passed on Dr Phillips' message, and immediately started murmuring to each other when she told them they were dismissed. But as they all walked back into the main reception area, they stopped dead in their tracks. Blocking their path was the most enormous bright red sack they had ever seen, tied up with festive green string at the top. Attached to it was a big light-brown label with the words *For The Children. Merry Christmas* written in big blue letters. It was literally bursting at the seams.

Jenny thought she heard hurried footsteps in the distance and the sound of the lift door closing, but she ignored it. A big grin grew from ear to ear as an enormous sense of relief rushed through her body – he had remembered. She looked at her watch – two minutes to midnight.

'He didn't forget. I told you so!' she exclaimed merrily. 'Come on, help me with them – we only have a few hours.'

The other nurses were staring wide-eyed and open-mouthed, having never seen anything like it before; the sack was so huge it had a kind of comedic farcicality to it. All kinds of questions were racing around in their heads. For one thing, it was clearly way too big for any of them to carry and looked unbelievably heavy. Whoever, or whatever, had carried the sack here so quickly was undoubtedly quite a scary character.

James seemed to recover before the others.

'But, how did he … it … get … did anyone see anything? Call secu…'

'That's quite enough, thank you,' Jenny intercepted, 'no one is calling anyone. I know it must be hard for you to understand an act of pure kindness when you see one, but just accept it and get stuck in. It'll be light before we know it.'

'I'm not trying to understand any act of kindness,' he managed, gawping at the immense bag, 'I'm just slightly worried about … about what carried it in here! Look at the size of it!'

Jenny had to admit he had a point. She had never really thought much about how he or she managed such a huge undertaking every year; whoever they were, all she cared about was how happy the children would be in the morning. So before they could all think about it too much, she untied the sack, which came open easily, and marvelled at the sight.

There were easily two hundred toys inside, each wrapped in a different type of paper so that it was easy to tell which ones were for the younger or older children. This was new; clearly more thought had gone into it this year. From past experience, Jenny knew that they would all be beautifully handcrafted wooden toys, unlike anything you could buy in the shops. Collectively, they looked like every child's ultimate dream. She pulled one out and looked at the label. It said *Merry Christmas. Now Get Better Quickly*. She looked over at the ward of sleeping children. Whoever had done this had managed to get this enormous heavy sack past them quietly

17

enough so as not to wake the children and then sneak out without being seen. Well, almost.

'Whoever you are, God bless you,' she said.

They all set about organising the presents into piles. Within minutes, the ward was silently buzzing with doctors and nurses who had heard about the mysterious Santa, and couldn't quite believe how he had done it again and managed to remain anonymous.

Chapter Two

The Ride

Downstairs, Dr Dawn Levvy walked Art through reception as quietly and as inconspicuously as possible.

'What did you tell them?' Art asked, as they walked past the café with its shutters down and its chairs turned upside down.

The shutters to the gift shop had a picture of a sunset in flaky paint, and a heavy chain and padlock was rooted to the ground holding it closed. It seemed everywhere in the hospital was closed, but every now and then, someone in a white coat or shirt and open collar with a stethoscope around their necks hurried past, and for every ten or fifteen yards they walked, a bored-looking person was sat at a large desk overlooking a virtually deserted waiting area. The windows all showed the same picture; the pitch-blackness of a very early dark and cold winter's morning, some of them with fake snow sprayed in circles on the inside. At some, branches covered in heavy frost pressed against the glass as if trying to get in.

'All I said was, Christmas Day is a time to be especially vigilant of anything out of the ordinary, and that all staff should be collectively reminded of that as soon as possible. Or something to that effect. Put it this way, they wouldn't have believed *me*, so I gave myself an instant promotion to the Board. We didn't want a repeat of three years ago, did we? I trust it worked?' Dr Levvy said, as she beamed down at Art.

'I thought at first it hadn't,' he said; 'nobody moved for quite a while. But then they all disappeared at once, so I dragged it quietly across the floor, left it in the usual place, grabbed a couple of mince pies and just managed to dart back inside the lift and head back down. Here you go.' Art handed Dawn the remaining mince pie, and she accepted it with a chuckle.

19

'The only easy bit was imitating the arrogance of that old coot. I wish he could have heard it.'

'Thanks, Dr Levvy,' said Art. 'I don't know how I'd do it without you.'

She looked at him with a puzzled look on her face.

'Don't thank me, for heaven's sake – what about all those children who will have some toys the moment they wake up?'

She put her hand on his shoulder as they reached the automatic doors.

'I don't know why you do it, Art, but thank you, from the bottom of my heart, *thank you*. I just wish you'd let people know it's you.'

Art shifted his feet, slightly embarrassed.

'I don't want people hassling me all the time at school and stuff. Anyway, I like making toys. I'm good at working with wood.'

It was true, he was. At a young age he had been given a plastic woodwork set with a big red saw, a big clumsy tape measure and several big plastic screwdrivers. Any other child would have been ecstatic about such a gift, but Art quickly realised that the saw didn't actually *cut* anything, however hard he tried, and that the clumsy screwdrivers were supposed to do something but he didn't know what. He quickly tired of the play set, because every time he played with it he got into trouble for sawing red plastic marks into the kitchen surfaces and leaving quite impressive dents in the fridge.

A couple of years later, when his knowledge of the world that was his house and garden grew and he became aware of the shed, he crept in one summer's day and got a glimpse of his dad's workbench. It was laden with different sized vices, neat piles of sandpaper, various chisels and real saws hanging on the wall, and real screwdrivers in a jar next to boxes full of screws and nuts and bolts. He knew instinctively what everything was for, and pictures of things to make came flooding into his mind from nowhere, along with an irresistible urge to try. To any normal little boy this would have been an awe-inspiring but nonetheless bewildering sight, but Art was no ordinary boy. Not by a long shot.

Ever since that day, he had been able to craft anything he wanted out of wood. It just seemed to come naturally. The very fabric of the wood fascinated him, calmed him and seemed to make him feel completely in control whenever he was working on it. The grain of the wood, the smell of the sawdust, the satisfaction of fitting pieces together that he hadn't checked would fit but just knew they would. Nothing seemed impossible when he was holding a finished toy or ornament. He often got back to his room just before bedtime with wooden cars and trucks, soldiers and swords, and once even with a sliding pencil case with hidden sweet compartments that nobody could find except him, no matter how hard they tried. The kitchen became full of beautifully crafted trays, chopping boards, noticeboards and all sorts of tools that were constantly in use, and always gratefully received, and the whole house with wooden frames, ornaments, garden tools and pails, all immaculate, all used, all wanted.

The trouble was that after a while he just didn't have any room for the rapidly growing pile of toys in his room, but he just couldn't bring himself to throw them away. He started painting and varnishing them all to try and slow down the production, but his room soon started to overflow with toys on every shelf and hanging from strings attached to the ceiling. So, just before Christmas at the tender age of nine, he decided to make some room in his closet for some of the new presents he had been promised if he was good, and on the way to school one morning he left an enormous sack of them in the hospital reception with a sign saying 'For The Children', and ran away as fast as he could.

The next day he was involved in an accident that permanently damaged his thumb and he had ended up on the Children's Ward himself. When Christmas morning came, he woke to find the set of wooden cars he had made the year before, still immaculately painted and shiny with varnish, in neat rows next to him on the bedside cabinet. He saw the other children playing with all sorts of other toys crafted by his own hand, many of whom Art was seeing smile for the first time. It had given him a warm feeling to

21

see his efforts make so many children happy, and ever since then he had made the toys with the express view of stockpiling them throughout the year and giving them to the hospital at Christmas. But every year it had become more and more difficult to drop them off without people seeing, and he was embarrassed about what he was doing. He didn't want people to know it was him, and every year he tried harder and harder to stay anonymous. Then, on the one year he thought his game would be up, the mysterious and slightly magical Maga had appeared, and every year since it had ceased being a chore and had become pure pleasure. Maga's company was joy personified, but his visits were all too short. He only saw him once a year, and it was never enough.

Art looked up at Dawn and shrugged his best fake shrug.

'Well, you're doing me a favour really. I need to get rid of them, and, well, someone may as well have them,' he said.

Dawn looked at him with a tight grin, not fooled for a second.

'Of course we're doing you a favour,' she said; 'we could always do with some excess toys lying around that you need to get rid of, and that just happen to be beautifully wrapped and labelled at exactly the right time of year. I know you too well, Art!' She hugged him, unable to contain her admiration any longer.

At that moment, a small black car drew up outside the double doors, hissed to a halt and sat there humming, smoothly. Dawn looked up at it, intrigued. It was the same strange vehicle that had picked Art up the last four years running. It was short and roundish, jet black, with blacked-out windows and very strange wheels and hubcaps. It looked like a big, very expensive toy, and sounded like a wind-up toy, with a little electrical hum over the top for good measure, and Dawn was sure that there was a bright yellow glow trying to escape from underneath the bonnet. The passenger door clicked loudly and then slowly hissed open. Dawn squinted to see who was inside, but the cabin was dark and the driver's face obscured. She gave Art a rather odd look.

22

'Are you sure this is your lift, Art?'

He looked out at the little humming car and gave a quick grin.

'Yes, that's it,' he said confidently.

The person in the little black car was Maga, the sprite who had mysteriously appeared when he had nearly missed his self-imposed midnight deadline a few years ago. He had told Art to meet him outside the main entrance then, as he was tonight. Art fondly remembered Maga's explanation as to why he had helped as he did.

'It's simply because of all this damn technology,' Maga had said. 'It's become harder and harder for you to go unnoticed and it's time we intervened. It's such a nice thing you're doing, and we couldn't let it stop. So Cinny and me,' the little car revved its engine up and down all on its own, 'were sent here to help. After all, I am the best field agent there is.' Maga puffed his chest out as he said this. And since then, Maga had turned up every year from among a crowd of statue-like people, greeted Art with an over-enthusiastic hug, taken him into a side office somewhere and explained the *real* plan in place of the one Dr Levvy always kindly came up with. And every year it got more and more complicated, as Maga produced more little stopper-bottles that did all sorts of amazing things. The most helpful of these was a strange liquid with a pinkish glow that looked solid in the bottle but drew up into the little dropper as easily as all the others, and made the ever-growing bag Art carried with him as light as a feather. For the last two years running, Maga had given him a large sack just slightly bigger than his usual black holdall that seemed to hold whatever Art filled it with. It seemed to get heavier and heavier, but never much bigger. On the drive home in the little black car, which seemed to drive itself, Maga would make another of those hot drinks for himself in his beat-up old tankard, and they'd talk about how the plan had worked, laughing and joking about the things that had nearly gone wrong, or the people they had managed to move into hilarious positions while still frozen in time. He couldn't wait to talk to Maga this year about the group of unmoving doctors he'd managed to draw beards and

23

moustaches on with a big black marker pen, and then how he'd placed the marker in the hand of the oldest-looking before whistling off around the corridor to the next checkpoint. *His visits are never long enough*, Art thought.

'I have to go now,' Art said, and hugged her goodbye for another year. Even though her plan was always usurped by Maga's, it was always reserved as a backup, and Art was grateful she was always there and so happy to help, whatever the cost.

Dawn looked at the little car and its secret driver again, and said, 'Now, you take care of yourself, young man, and have a good Christmas, do you hear?'

Art reached into his pocket, pulled out a small package wrapped in tissue paper and pressed it into her hand.

'I will,' he said; 'see you next year.'

He climbed into the passenger seat and closed the door with a smile for the doctor who helped him remain anonymous every year; then the little car pulled away. Dawn watched it disappear into the darkness as the automatic doors closed. She looked at the package in her hand. She opened the wrapping paper and found a small wooden replica of the hospital, with every detail carved and painted to perfection, right down to the caterpillars and ladybirds on the windows of the Children's Ward, and the lights that were always on on the top floor.

'Bless you, Art,' she said, and went up to the third floor to act as surprised as the rest of the nurses at the magical gift that was given to the Children's Ward every year.

Christmas Day finally arrived and most of the children were still asleep. Jenny walked down the row of beds, inspecting each pile of presents with military precision.

Any minute now, she thought, *one of them will wake up, and then they'll all be awake within seconds*. She chuckled to herself. She walked back to the

24

reception desk and was just taking a swig of tea when, sure enough, she heard the first little shriek, then another. After the third, a cacophony broke out. Jenny put on her mental riot gear and ran into the thick of it.

Chapter Three

Elfee

'Hurry up, Jack, we'll be late! Well, even later than we are already... Oh, I can't believe we overslept!'

Jackie, Evi's mother, rushed down the hallway, putting on her coat as she shouted up the stairs. Evi was standing at the door ready to go, as she had been for the last five minutes, cool as a cucumber. Jack, Evi's father, hurried down the stairs with shaving foam around his ears carrying a plastic sack full of presents with a tacky-looking Santa's face on it.

'Don't worry, dear, I'm ready when you are,' Jackie said.

They hurried out of the door, and Evi followed.

'Have you got all of them, dear?' said Jackie, a hint of panic in her voice.

'Yes, the lot – the Action Soldier Rigid Raider, that big robot thingy and all of the stocking presents. Relax, love.'

Evi smirked. Relax! They couldn't relax if they tried.

Jack and Jackie rushed to the car as Evi clicked the front door shut behind them with no sense of urgency. She knew there was no point in rushing.

'Have you got the car keys, dear?' asked Jackie.

'No, you've got them, haven't you?'

'I haven't got them – oh, let me look in my handbag – I know I haven't got them.' She rummaged around frantically in her bag. 'You see, dear? They're not here ... you must have them somewhere. Oh, here they are!'

Evi had walked towards the car at a normal pace, and by the time her parents had finished panicking, tried to open the door with the key to the shed and found the car key, the car was unlocked just in time for her to coolly open the rear door and casually sit down. She swung the door shut as

Jack started the car, and they pulled away with a jerk, stalled, restarted and pulled away again with way too many revs and a cloud of smoke. Evi closed her eyes – it was better that way. The ride was fast and clumsy, and she decided it was better not to look.

They arrived at the hospital, parked at an angle so that the car took up two spaces and exited, two frantically, one not. Jack and Jackie rushed towards the entrance and disappeared from view. Evi walked over to the ticket machine, bought a ticket (saving her parents a hefty fine), displayed it on the dashboard, locked the car and made it through the main entrance with plenty of time to look at the hospital map, find the Children's Ward, casually call to her parents who were still ringing the bell at the reception desk for someone to tell them where to go and walked towards the first elevator, three turns down the corridor. Her parents rushed past her, got lost and she caught up, then they rushed away again, and so it continued until they eventually found the right corridor.

The doors to the Children's Ward burst open and two red-faced parents puffed through, followed by a nonplussed teenage girl. Nurse Hopkins heard the commotion and got up to intervene.

'Where's my little Nathan?' came Jackie's cry.

'Oh, you must be Mr and Mrs Wise,' said Jenny. 'Nathan's in Ladybird Ward, bed 4.'

Jack and Jackie rushed past, while Evi introduced herself.

'I'm Nathan's sister, Evi,' she said. 'I'm sorry we're late, especially on Christmas morning, but we overslept. You see, Nathan usually gets us up on Christmas morning, as you can probably imagine.'

Jenny chuckled. 'Yes, I can imagine; he's quite a character. He's just over there – bed 4.'

'Thank you,' Evi smiled.

She walked in the direction of the right ward, expecting to see a rather upset little boy; after all, the other parents were here already and had no doubt showered their little offspring with Christmas presents by now. She was wishing she had set an alarm for herself when she caught sight of him. His face was bright and happy, and he was totally lost in a bath of glittery wrapping paper. He was not the broken little boy she was expecting. He was holding a shiny red truck with black wheels and a little man in the cabin, and was loading the last of the yellow numbered bricks into the back. He pulled a handle and the number one brick popped out. He pulled it again and the number two brick popped out. Then the three and the four, then...

'NATHAN!' Jack and Jackie shouted, and rushed over to their little boy.

He was overjoyed to see them. He received a combined hug from both of them, and was quite painfully squashed by his mother.

Evi walked over.

'Hey, squidge,' she said, and hugged him too. 'Happy Christmas!'

They all sat round while Nathan opened his toys, including those from Santa. First came the little robot with the remote control wand, and after much dilly-dallying from Jack in reading the instructions, Nathan quickly worked out on his own how to make it snatch the booklet from his father and spin around dancing. Next came some of the stocking presents – the ones he was supposed to open the moment he opened his eyes on Christmas morning. There were lots of funny coloured pens and colouring books, little cars that raced around in circles on his hospital tray, several figures that transformed into trees (all the rage, apparently) and way too many chocolate coins to be healthy. And finally, at the bottom of the sack, came the Action Soldier Rigid Raider. This caused the most commotion, because it was the most exciting of his presents but the hardest to get into. There was clear plastic at the front of the box and they could all see the figure sitting in the rather mean-looking assault boat, but after several failed attempts to get the box open, they found that he was strapped in using metal wire on each of his limbs and his neck. In the end, a rather heavy pair of surgical scissors was called for over the phone, and the soldier was freed. Nathan couldn't believe his luck. The Action Soldier had several different weapons and could use all of them while sitting in his boat, using his free hand to control the vessel. At

28

least that's what Nathan told them. To his complete surprise there was a little button inside the cockpit that turned on the propeller at the back. It could actually go in the water! But he would have to wait until he was out of hospital and back home before he could use this in the bath.

Evi was feeling very happy that Nathan had cheered up so much. She was very close to her little brother and didn't like to see him upset. Even though he had been very happy with all his presents, she noticed that the truck he had been playing with when they arrived was never very far away. Every time he opened something new, she noticed that out of the corner of his eye he always checked to make sure the little truck was still there. Once or twice, if it was too long between presents arriving, she noticed that he actually reached for it in favour of almost everything else he had been given. He was busy telling his dad about the devastation the Rigid Raider's weapons could cause, so Evi reached for his truck. It was immaculate, and so smooth that it took her a while to notice it was made of wood. The finish was machine-like, and the paint shiny and unblemished. The little driver in the cabin was quite simple to look at, but when the wheels went round his head turned from left to right, although Evi couldn't see any joints or holes that linked the head to the wheels. When she looked more closely at the cabin, she realised there were no joins anywhere. The whole cabin must have been carved out of one piece of wood, driver and all. The attention to detail was incredible, right down to the tread on the tyres. No factory worker had made this – it was the product of an artisan of unrivalled skill, and Evi had never seen anything like it.

She looked around the ward. Every child had similar toys amongst their Christmas presents, and none of them were forgotten for long, their presence being checked periodically. They were all immaculate, shiny and smooth, and there were so many different types: mini doll's prams with beautiful dolls in them that didn't look as though they could be made of wood, racing cars with little drivers gripping the steering wheels as if they were driving for their lives, several friendly looking robots with shiny silver limbs and piercing red eyes, and an assortment of farm animals, whistles and spinning tops. And none of them were cast aside or forgotten.

Evi walked over to the reception desk where Jenny was sitting watching all the festivities. She noticed Evi holding the truck.

'Beautiful, isn't it?' she said. 'The kids love those toys so much.'

'Where do they come from?' asked Evi, an inquisitive look on her face.

'That's the mystery,' said Jenny; 'no one really knows. The children wake up on Christmas morning surrounded by them, but no one knows where they come from.'

Evi had read about this in the local paper a few years ago, and had become interested in who would do such a thing. She had long since lost faith in the human race, and found it hard to believe there was still *anyone* around who genuinely cared about others, at least not without some ulterior motive. She hadn't quite believed the news column, but was secretly hoping there was some truth in it. Year after year the paper reported a similar incident, always at the same time of year, and her faith had grown slightly each time, but never quite enough to believe any *one* person was involved with nothing to gain but personal satisfaction. But now she had experienced it first-hand and she was more than intrigued. She decided there and then to discover who was behind it, at all costs.

'You really don't know who it is? But how do they get in here?' Evi said.

'Well,' started Jenny, 'every year on Christmas Eve, usually close to midnight, some kind of distraction happens to drag us all away, usually for just a moment. And when we get back, they're just … *there*, right in front of us. Heaven knows how they get there.'

'And you know nothing about it, of course?' remarked Evi.

Jenny shifted slightly. 'What do you mean?' she said.

'Well, if I were you,' Evi continued, 'I'd be slightly worried about the security implications of that. I mean, if he can get in here without being seen or heard, anyone could, couldn't they?'

30

Jenny looked slightly troubled. 'I'm sure I don't know what you mean. I take very good care of the children, thank you very much.'

Evi smiled. 'I'm sure you do,' she said. Out of the corner of her eye she noticed the model hospital sitting on the desk. She made a mental note and returned to Nathan's bedside, where he was waiting for his truck.

The special extended visiting hours for Christmas drew to a close as the windows grew darker and darker. Nearly everyone was wearing a paper hat of some description, although most were crumpled or torn after a day's use. Jenny sighed, looked over the babble of excited children and parents, and rose from her seat. She took off her paper crown, crumpled it up and threw it into the bin beside her, and started towards the first bed. A few minutes later she reached bed 4.

'I'm ever so sorry, but we really must ask you to make a move. You can come back first thing tomorrow, but for now, visiting time is over.'

They all thanked her and began gathering up their belongings. Evi picked up her handbag and then glanced over her shoulder to check the nurse had moved on. Without making a sound, she glided over to the reception desk and scanned the surface. Nothing. She looked over her shoulder and quickly slipped into the doctor's office. Inside was a large untidy desk with a brass nameplate which read Dr D Levvy. She scanned the items on the desk and quickly found the little model hospital. She picked it up and saw that it was crafted in the same perfect hand as all the other toys. Evi thought it a bit odd that the mysterious Santa would give one of the doctors something too. It was confirming her suspicions that the nurse knew more than she was letting on. Evi turned it upside down. The underneath was perfectly smooth, bar a strange insignia carved into one corner and a small inscription neatly carved into the other: *Thanks for all your help. Arthur.*

There was only one Arthur she knew of – a very strange boy she had met but never spoken to on her first day at the new school. He had stared at her for the whole of the first day, and later she had found out he was childhood friends with her best friend Tina. Every time she saw him he had been

31

helping someone with something, or talking to a very large frightening-looking boy who was often alone and sad. He kept himself to himself and wasn't very popular, but she had never seen anything but kindness when she looked at him. And even though he was nothing special to look at, she found herself looking at him a lot, though it usually meant that he would walk into something or drop what he was carrying. In the end, Evi thought it would be kinder not to look at him so much, for his own sake. The thought of him made her smile.

'Arthur Elfee. I *knew* it!'

She replaced the little model in exactly the same spot and rejoined her family.

Dialogue One

'Jimma – activity in the portal. Processing. Small vehicle, one occupant. No possessions or contraband. It has a Level 1 clearance. Shall I let it pass?'

'No, give me a look at it. Level 1s are good at concealing things beyond the initial scan. I'm going to run a close-quarters filter and look inside his pockets. Literally. We've had trouble with this one before.'

'Jimma, will you stop this charade? You know full well who he is, and you know we can't touch him even if we do find something. The order comes right from the Boss. He goes through.'

'I know that, Pud, but don't forget that I have more Gold Stars than you. If I want to check inside his pockets, I will. Is that clear?'

'Okay, okay, you're the boss, just because you've been working here for a couple of decades more than me. Big deal. Very well, oh Four-Gold-Starred One, let your slightest wish be my command. Would thee like one's nose blown? May I make thee a stroth brew? How about a couple of dough drops to go with it?'

'Listen, Pud, this is the fourth trip he's made this month. I know the order came right from the Boss, I took it down myself. He gave him guaranteed, unquestioned passage, and immunity should we find anything on him. But nowhere on the order did it say we weren't allowed to look for anything, did it? Have you ever wondered where he goes and why it's always to the same place? No one ever goes to the same place more than once a year, but he goes through once a week. Come on, don't tell me you're not the slightest bit curious.'

'Well, hmm, erm ... well, I don't ... oh okay, let's have a look. He's not moving linearly is he?'

'He has no idea we're even having this conversation.'

33

'Okay, let's punch it up.'

'Now you're talking! Bring up the schematic. Filter through the doors, that's it; right, zoom in there, let's look at his top pockets. Right one first. Closer, zero the filter to that spot. A little to the left, up a bit, left a bit more ... right, hit the button.'

'Nothing. Just his pass and a few pastry crumbs. Pass has expired. Can't touch him. Next pocket?'

'Go for it. Zero in to that spot and...'

'Yes, thank you, Jimma, I can work the console you know. Zeroed and ready.'

'Hit the button.'

'Nothing. Oh hang on, what's that? Scan says it's wooden. Very faint image – looks like a figure of some kind. Key ring d'ya reckon? I don't see any metal loops.'

'What would he want with a key ring? Still, it's not exactly contraband – nothing to worry about. Next pocket.'

'Right bottom?'

'No, try the inside pockets. They're usually the sweetest catch.'

'Bit more tricky – I'll have to filter the top pockets right out ... give me a second. Right, zeroed and ready.'

'Hit the button.'

'Bingo! Two cloth pouches, half empty, one nearly full vile. Dear, dear, didn't even bother to dump the rest before he came through. Sloppy work, Jimma.'

'What's in the first?'

'Hang on, analysing. Nearly there ... here it is. Printing. First one's through.'

'Okay, give it here. Ah, haven't seen this for a while. Reconnaissance Chocolate. Someone doesn't want to be seen. Why on earth would he want to use that? Unless he... Pud, I have the feeling we shouldn't really be looking at this stuff. The Boss is usually the only one who uses...'

34

'Second one's through.'

'Memory Bubbles. I don't like this, it's highly classified stuff we're looking at. Pud, as the holder of Four Gold Stars I...'

'Third one's through. That's the lot.'

'Anonymity Toffees. Pud, clear the filter. Unpatch the schematic and give him his clearance.'

'Why? Isn't it our job to at least look at the things people bring through?'

'In this instance, I would say no. Definitely not, no. The Boss is the only one who has need of this stuff, and he's very picky about who makes it for him. His methods are extremely secret. Even the manufacturers are ordered to forget what it is they've just made. Everyone believes it's just a rumour, even the ones who make the stuff. Trust me, Pud, we should not be looking at this stuff. Give him his clearance and let him through. Now.'

'Okay, unpatching. Linear movement resumed at one quarter ... he's through. Shall I file the report?'

'No, wipe it. Wipe it all. Cup of stroth brew would be nice.'

'But, Jim...'

'Two drops of honey, Pud.'

'Oh come o...'

'Dough drops, Pud, don't forget the dough drops.'

Chapter Four

The Incredible Day

The front door clicked open and Art slipped through. With careful precision he slowly clicked it shut again and re-deadlocked it. In the shady moonlit gloom he made out four glowing green eyes staring at him. They were exactly where he had left them when he had crept out hours before.

'Hey, Speedy, Steph,' he whispered. His two faithful Beagles sat motionless on the hall mat. He tiptoed over and kneeled down in front of them. 'It's okay, I'm back now. Nothing to it. You guys can relax.'

With these words they silently broke rank and rushed up to him, wagging their tails and quietly woofing, almost under their breath.

'Well done, guys. Hey, calm down, okay? Relax.'

He scratched them both behind the ears, then stood to make his way up to his room. He looked up the gloomy flight of stairs and cocked his head to listen.

'Hear anything, guys?'

Steph and Speedy had fallen back in rank behind him as if to guard him as he went. He felt to his side and patted Steph's head, then shifted his weight to lift up his leg. Just as his foot touched the first step, Steph made an almost inaudible woof. Art froze.

At the top of the stairs, a door to the right of the landing creaked open and a small figure stumbled across into the bathroom. It was Art's little brother Walt. The door closed and Art could make out the rustling of clothes, the flushing of the toilet and then the door opened again. Halfway across the landing, Walt stopped and looked down the stairs. The steps curved round at the bottom and Art was just out of sight. He took a step towards the edge to get a better look, then walked back into his room and closed the door behind him.

Art edged slowly up the stairs, avoiding all the creaky areas, and glided across the landing to his own room. The handle turned easily and silently, and Art slid through the gap, allowing enough room for Speedy and Steph to trot silently in behind him and head for their beds.

Art's room was filled with shelf after shelf of toys, each one gleaming in the light from his bedside lamp. Every wall had at least seven rows of shelves and every inch of each one was filled with something brightly coloured and shining. Some had toys hanging from string or long wooden arms, and Christmas toys of every description were interspersed, lit up by a string of different coloured lights. The whole room had a very festive, snug feel to it.

Art silently shut the door behind him, and two small red lights on the wall lit up with an almost inaudible low beep. Steph and Speedy were already in their baskets settling down for a well-earned sleep as Art crossed the room to his bed. Some of the toys on the shelves were moving up and down or spinning on little spindles, throwing dancing shadows across the walls. Art took off his black hooded top and threw it somewhere he might find it in the morning. He was just unbuckling his belt when he felt something in his pocket. He fished it out. It was a small box wrapped in paper. Art clicked on his small bedside light. Across the room, four green eyes sprang open and then shut again just as quickly. Art examined the gift and wondered how it had got there. The box was small, easily small enough for a thimble, and was made of a very hard green cardboard material; the lid was sealed shut with a small band of white tape emblazoned with a strange sort of spiral-heart shape, with a vertical tail drawn in red along its length. It looked strangely familiar. He turned the box over, but nowhere could he see where the tape ended. It was one continuous loop. Art rummaged in his bedside cabinet drawer for his red Swiss Army knife and opened the largest blade, slipped it flat under the tape and forced the sharp edge into it. It

37

bulged, but did not cut. Art started sawing at it, but the tape only moved slightly with the motions of the blade. Art put the knife down and started feeling around the tape with his finger to try to find a seam, but as he did so, it loosened under his fingers and fell to the floor. Turning his attention back to the box, he lifted the tiny lid.

Inside, on a tiny cushion of deep red felt, rested a small silver amulet. It was no bigger than an old halfpence but twice as thick, and in the shape of a teardrop. On the front, the same symbol as on the tape was ornately carved, and the grooves were a strange colour, in fact lots of colours that seemed to change as he moved the box. In the thinnest part of the teardrop was a small hole, and Art noticed that the amulet was threaded onto a piece of old dark brown twine. He reached inside and gently lifted out the amulet, letting the twine uncoil until it was completely out of the box. It was surprisingly heavy for such a small object, and seemed even thicker now. Along the edges were strange markings, like a dialect he couldn't decipher. He stared at it intently, wondering what it was, and as he did so he got an overwhelming urge to slip the twine over his head and wear it like a pendant. He separated the circle of twine between his fingers and moved it slowly up towards him, but as it moved closer, the amulet started vibrating. Art was startled by this and put it down quickly on his bedside cabinet. He stood very still, wondering what had happened, then reached out and put it back in its box, closing the lid. He reached down and picked up the white tape, but found that it would no longer fit around the box. He tried several times, but it was too small, as if it had never been big enough in the first place. He put them both inside his top drawer and decided to try to forget about them until the morning.

The Christmas holidays were always some of the best days of Art's life, his very favourite time of the year. He loved the decorations and lights everywhere, the whole CD collection put away and replaced with Christmas music played back to back all day, and best of all, no telly in the evening, which would usually mortify Art and his little brother Walt. But Christmas holidays were very special, and evening meals were made up of leftovers from the ridiculously huge Christmas dinner, and seemed to flow effortlessly into a session of cards around the table with the whole family. Mum and Dad, Grandma and Granddad, sometimes an uncle and aunt or two, and sometimes Art's best friend Tina, but always Christmas music, plenty of crisps and fizzy drinks, and the oblivious passage of time. Art and Walt barely noticed their beloved telly at all. And that's how it was until the end of the holidays; from writing their letters to Santa and sending them burning up the chimney, through to New Year, when the decorations were reluctantly taken down, again with endless crisps and fizzy drink and a last listen to the Christmas music. Then everyone said goodnight with sadness in their hearts, but ready for another eleven months of normal life. Art tried to pretend he was looking forward to watching the telly again, but he was only fooling himself. He had even forgotten about Maga, whom he wished he could share it all with every day. Maga seemed to make everything more fun than it could be on its own, and Art knew his family would warm to him. But he knew he could never mention him to anyone; Maga had made that absolutely clear. His visits were strictly confidential, and apart from anything else, what would his family make of him? It had taken Art a while to come to terms with the origin of his strange little sprite friend, and he still wasn't even sure what a sprite was. He decided that Maga was right, that he should remain a secret, at least for now.

The next morning, Art rushed Walt out of the door for school, remembering just in time to snatch the key hanging from a rope on the hook above the kitchen door and throw it around his neck underneath his uniform. Some people felt sorry for Art and Walt being latchkey kids, but in truth, Art loved it. As soon as the house was parent-free in the mornings, Walt would change channel on the telly as Art poured them both another helping of cereal. They would sit and watch the 'grown-up' cartoons, crunching loudly, usually remembering just in time to leave for school. Art clicked the gate shut as he stepped onto the pavement, and a large group of Walt's friends

39

called out for him from across the street. Walt waved, but made no move to join them. Art knew Walt's friends taunted him for having an 'un-trendy' brother, but Walt was ferociously loyal and defended him relentlessly. But being rather cool himself, it never affected his credibility, and apart from this one collective character defect they were a good circle of friends for Walt.

Art chuckled. 'Off you go, little bro, don't wait around for me,' he said, and gave Walt a friendly little shove.

Walt gave his brother a quick grin, then ran to the crossing. Art pulled his earphones from his top pocket and turned his music up to a loud but bearable level. Stravinsky was his favourite, but Art considered himself lucky that he could appreciate so many different types of music. Today his head was filled with big band jazz. Heaven forbid if Walt's friends found out about the 'drivel' he was listening to.

The main road to school was very cheerful, even in the winter, with its pavements lit up by the light coming through the empty trees parading on both sides for its entire length. As Art walked past the many houses on this side of the street, his grandma's was easily the most recognisable of them all, with its bright pink walls, red window shutters and green roof. Most of the street thought it rather bilious, but Art liked it. All year round the little front garden was full of various flowers in full bloom, long after everyone else's had withered with the cold. Three hundred and sixty-five days of the year, Grandma Elfee's garden was awash with colour, much to the envy and confusion of the whole town. Quite how she did it no one knew, but her secret was closely guarded. Art glanced towards the house as he passed and saw Grandma Elfee staring at him from one of the upstairs windows. She smiled at him and pointed to the postbox fixed to the gatepost. Art stopped next to it and pulled open the little door. Inside was a clear plastic tub with two slices of fruit cake topped with bright blue icing resting on a neatly folded napkin. Art smiled and took out the box. He placed it in his bag and smiled up at the window. Grandma Elfee waved and disappeared from view. There was simply nothing like one of her cakes, and Art could feel the tub was still warm in his hands. With it safely packed away, he continued the walk to school.

Outside the gates, Art caught up with Walt who was waiting for him as he did every morning.

'Hey, scruff bag. Where's the gang?' Art sang, as he reached into his bag for the cake.

'They're okay really,' Walt defended; 'they're just slaves to fashion and all things cool. They've rushed in to see the twins' new phones – can't resist a bit of new tech.'

Art opened the tub and handed Walt a piece of the cake.

'Don't forget we're at Grandma's for tea tonight,' he said.

'Oh, I haven't forgotten – she's got Death Ray III for the Puu console with the rifle controllers and everything. I hope she doesn't beat me this time. Still, the food's always good,' he said, his mouth a shower of crumbs. He could never wait for break time to eat one of his grandma's cakes, and he spoke with a shower of crumbs. 'So, we'll be walking home with Tina and Evi tonight then?'

Grandma's house was next door to Evi Wise, the girl whose looks had dazzled Art since he'd arrived at St David's Comprehensive. His best friend Tina, whom he'd known since his first day of school, was a good friend of Evi's, and the two of them were inseparable during school hours. Even after school, they would be in and out of each other's houses all evening. Theirs was a very strange relationship – Evi was in with the cool and fashionable half of the school, while Tina was a computer geek with as much dress sense as Art. But when Evi had arrived at the school during their third year with not a familiar face in sight, Tina had been the first to walk up to her with a smile and offer to show her around for the day. Evi had never forgotten her kindness, and whatever label schoolchildren insisted on giving one another, it never mattered – Evi and Tina were firm friends from that day on. But recently, whenever Art was with them, Tina would find convenient reasons to be doing something elsewhere, and she'd sidle off with a sideways grin on

41

her face, taking sly glances over her shoulder as she went. Of course, whenever that happened Art would have no idea what to say to Evi, and once, when he had tried to say he thought she looked nice, the boiled sweet in his mouth had plopped out and stuck to his school jumper, staining it with a big purple mark that had never come out. Still, it could have been worse – it could have stuck to *her* school jumper. Art was grateful for that bit of good luck.

'Yes, we are,' said Art, jabbing Walt in the ribs to make him laugh.

Walt spat an even bigger spray of crumbs and darted out of the way just too late. He laughed and started making kissing sounds as he ran off to his classroom.

'See you after school, stinky!' Art shouted after him, and hurried off in the opposite direction.

Art sat at his desk, early as usual for double science. He had opened one of his many notebooks and was doodling on one of the middle pages absent-mindedly. Art had a thing for notebooks. Every time he saw a new design in the stationers he had the urge to buy it. There was something about the new empty pages that fascinated him. Art was thinking about the walk home from school today when out of nowhere Tina slumped into the seat next to him and slapped a piece of paper over his doodle.

'Not bad; bit shaky at the beginning, and the less said about the ending the better, but the main body's not too bad at all. I guess you were joking when you said that sugar is used to make lemonade froth out of the glass, right?' she said.

Tina had been helping Art with his essay writing. As a student, Art was decidedly average, and Tina had taken it upon herself to tutor him in all the lessons they shared, which was pretty much all of them. She'd insisted on seeing his chemistry essay before he handed it in, which Art was secretly thankful for. Over the print on the page she'd written *Content C-, Effort A+* in red felt-tip. Art picked the sheet up and looked it over.

'Wow, thanks! I've never had a C before.' Tina looked at the strange shapes drawn over and over again in Art's notebook.

'Whoa. You still drawing that Goth design? She leaned a bit closer, noticing a change in the shape she'd seen him drawing before. 'It kind of looks like a heart now, don't you think?'

Art looked at it again. 'Yeah, I suppose so. I still don't really know why I keep drawing it. It just flows out whenever I doodle.'

'Yeah right,' Tina mocked.

'What does that mean?' Art asked.

'It's nearly the New Year's Ball and you...' (she sung this bit) 'want to take Evi...'

'That's got nothing to do with it,' Art lied; 'it's just I've seen this shape recently, on a little box I got something in for Christmas, and it's sort of heart-shaped. I hadn't noticed before.'

Art hadn't set out to draw the shape he had seen on the white tape from the box in his room, but it had happened naturally anyway, as if this was what he had meant to draw all along. He thumbed through some previous pages of old drawings, and the shape he saw just looked wrong.

'Of course it is, Art,' she said sarcastically. 'I believe you, ga-zillions wouldn't. Anyway, back to your essay. The bit in your conclusion about, and I quote, "bottom-burps" ... I know the essay is about gaseous pressure, but I wouldn't include that.'

'That came from a very reliable source,' Art protested. 'Walt said that...' and at that moment Art's teacher strode in.

She was a very athletic-looking woman, quite tall with long blonde hair swept back into a ponytail. She was in her late forties, but carried her age well – most of the fifth-year boys secretly had a crush on her. She was not really your stereotypical science teacher, and would often turn up as a sort of assistant teacher during PE lessons, where all the oldest boys would suddenly become very interested in the lesson. Also, Art knew she was an

43

excellent bassoon player, and attended every rehearsal and concert of the school band.

'Essays – I shall hand them back and I expect the next assignment in return,' she boomed. 'On the whole, not too bad. Adams, Brooke...'

She started handing the essays back as she walked idly around the classroom. Art liked Mrs Jones. She always taught every student as if they were as important as the last, and no one ever felt stupid in her class. Art's essay on the carbon cycle eventually landed on his desk with a big D-written in red pen at the bottom. Mrs Jones looked at him reassuringly. He had seen that look plenty of times before and it always meant the same thing – I know you tried hard, but still missing the point. This was the reason Art always got good school reports – his grades were never brilliant, but he always listened and tried hard in every class, and all the teachers knew it. They all knew him by name, and Art always felt more comfortable talking to them, as if they were meant to be his peer group.

Art noticed Mrs Jones putting an essay down on the desk of a very thickset boy called Peter. He was a very overweight lad due to his addiction to strawberry bonbons, and very mean-looking. On meeting him for the first time, most people were scared silly, and the youngsters in the school would squeal and run off in the opposite direction. But Art knew this boy very well. Peter had moved into the area only a couple of years ago, and spent his first day at school being avoided by everyone. At lunchtime, Art had gone back to his form-tutor room to get some books he had been asked to fetch and had found Peter sitting at a desk in the corner. He had the same angry expression on his face, but Art noticed some tears running down his cheek. He was eating strawberry bonbons out of a white paper bag and sniffing occasionally. Art's chest suddenly began to ache with an insane amount of sympathy for the huge, angry-looking boy crying silently to himself, and it was too much for him to bear. He went over and sat down next to him. Peter noticed Art out of the corner of his eye, and immediately offered him a bonbon. And, as Art found out, that action was typical of Peter's whole

44

character. Generous through and through, kind, one of life's real good guys. His appearance was probably the most deceiving of anyone he had ever met. He turned out to be Art's next best friend, but he still remained mostly unpopular at school; most people could not see past his terrifying appearance, all except Walt, who had never shown the slightest fear towards him.

Peter picked up his paper and saw the large D grade staring back at him. He put it down again and said nothing. Art knew Peter was under a lot of pressure from his dad to do well at school, and this latest grade would not go down well when he got home. Art looked on with the same ache of sympathy he had always had for Peter, and made up his mind to speak to him as soon as class was finished.

Art sat back and got ready for a long ninety minutes of science, although if he was honest, the biology side of these lessons was something he enjoyed. He reached into his coat pocket and sneakily popped a cola cube into his mouth. Then he leant over sideways to get his textbook from his bag, and as he did so the cake box caught his eye. There was something lying in the bottom that he had missed; it looked like a letter. He quietly ripped the lid off the box and dug whatever it was out. It *was* a letter, written on very old parchment and folded into four. Art opened it and froze at what he saw. In the top left corner was the same strange insignia he had found on the little box the night before; the same insignia Art was now drawing, with its distinctive heart shape. He nearly choked on his cola cube, and was so confused that he almost forgot to read the letter. It was a short note from Grandma explaining that she needed to speak privately with him that evening, and that he should rush home as soon as he could. Apparently, she had something she wanted to give him. Art folded the letter and put it away; he was unable to concentrate after that.

When the bell finally rang for morning break, Art picked up his stuff and headed for the door, forgetting to say goodbye to Tina. On his way past Peter's table, he dropped the bag of remaining cola cubes into his lap and wandered out of the classroom, lost in thought. He stumbled into the corridor and turned right, going nowhere in particular. The insignia on the letter had him totally dumbfounded and his mind was all over the place. What did it mean? Did the strange pendant have anything to do with Grandma? It didn't make any sense.

Art turned at the end of the now deserted corridor and collided with someone coming in the other direction. He immediately wished he'd been paying attention as all of Evi's books dropped to the floor, but Art was fixed to the spot in shock. Her shoulder-length black hair and beautiful brown eyes seemed to reduce him to nothing more than a statue, and as usual, he lost all power of speech and thought.

'Oh, I'm sorry,' she said, 'I didn't see you coming, and...'

She recognised Art and smiled at him warmly.

'Oh, it's you,' she said.

Art tried to say something, but all that came out was something that sounded like 'Brumble mum-tueees'. Evi knelt down to pick up her books, and Art attempted to help.

'I meant to talk to you actually,' she said, standing up with all her books cradled in one arm. 'I was at the hospital over Christmas,' she said. 'Nathan had broken his arm.' She paused to gauge Art's reaction.

Art was glad of his inability to speak, and she carried on.

'Something very strange had happened when we got there. All the children were playing with the most amazing toys we'd ever seen. Nat still has his, actually.' She paused again; still no response.

She reached into her bag, pulled out a slightly crumpled copy of the local paper and held it up for him to read. In the bottom corner of the front page was a small picture of some children in their hospital beds, all holding very brightly coloured toys up in the air and smiling for the cameraman. The headline read *N.H.S.ANTA STRIKES AGAIN*.

'I saw one of those toys – it had an inscription on it from someone called Arthur.' She paused, then said quietly, 'It's you, isn't it?'

46

Art was surprised by the directness of the question and snapped out of his stupor. He thought as quickly as he could, but nothing seemed to come to mind - he may as well have been in his stupor again. She moved closer to him and he felt dizzy looking into her eyes.

'I know it's you, Art. I *will* find out why you do it, you'll tell me on Thursday night.'

Art thought quickly – something was happening Thursday night? Then he remembered – it was the night of the New Year's Ball. *What did she mean by that?* Art thought. Just then a group of Evi's friends walked round the corner and spotted her.

'Evi, what are you doing talking to *that*?' said the tallest.

Evi didn't shift her gaze from Art.

'I'm asking him to the ball of course,' she replied, and the whole group erupted into hysterical laughter. But Evi's face still had the same kind smile she had worn for the last few minutes. As the crowd became uncomfortably near, she whispered, 'Pick me up at seven.'

Then she was swept away with her peers and Art heard the tall dark-haired girl say with laughter in her voice, 'That was cruel, Evi,' and she held up her hand for a high-five.

To Art's amazement, Evi gave her the most angry stare he had ever seen, and the tall girl pulled her hand back down quickly with a puzzled look on her face.

As the crowd disappeared around the corner, Art was left wondering what had just happened. Had Evi really just asked him to the ball or was it some sick joke? And if it was, why was she so angry at her friend for making fun of him? And how was it that she had an inkling he was behind the presents at Christmas? *I don't write on any of the toys*, he thought, *they're all leftovers. The only thing I inscribed was ... oh!* He remembered the present he had given to Dawn, but he couldn't believe she would have given him up so easily.

Today had been very confusing, and Art just wanted to get the rest of it over with and go home. But then he remembered his grandma's request and his brain became so muddled he thought it would explode. He was almost deafened as the bell rang right next to his ear, and he headed off in the direction of his next class, wondering if the day had any more surprises in store.

Chapter Five

The Gift

At the end-of-school bell, Art stuffed all his books into his bag, slung it onto his shoulder and hurried out of class. He headed down the corridor towards the front of the school and noticed a very large gap in the students a few feet in front of him; Peter was in the middle, being avoided by as many people as possible. Art pushed through those in front of him (they didn't put up much of a fight) and started walking beside him.

'Hey, Peter. Sucks about the Ds, doesn't it?'

'Yeah, dude,' he replied. 'Thanks for those cola cubes. Won't stop me getting grounded though.'

Art tried to put his arm around Peter's shoulder, but could only reach as far as the middle of his back.

'Well,' said Art, 'let's try and stop that happening again, shall we? What are your favourites again, bonbons? I've got a whole bag of lemon ones with your name on it if you help me plan for our exams. What do you say?'

Peter's face screwed up. '*Lemon* bonbons?'

'Yeah sorry, the shop's out of strawberry ones.'

'Eeugh,' Peter said. 'Okay then. When were you thinking?'

Art knew Peter was good with facts if he assigned each one to a different type of food as a reminder. It didn't help Art at all, but he really wanted Peter to do well – he couldn't bear to see him sad. Art knew only Tina could help him with his essay planning, and he'd lose that time if he spent it with Peter, but he couldn't stand the feeling he got in the pit of his stomach if he didn't try and help someone who needed it.

'After school tomorrow. Are you allowed study partners round if you're grounded?'

'Yeah, I think so,' said Peter.

'Good, I'll walk home with you then. Gotta go find Walt now. See you tomorrow, bonbon boy,' Art said, as he ran off down the corridor.

Peter laughed, but this only made him look even angrier and a few of the first-year students squealed and ran away.

Art rounded the corner of the last corridor, but just as the main entrance was coming into view a sharp pain shot through his wrist. He cried out and fell to the floor, overcome by the sudden sensation, and the contents of his bag spilled out around him. He grabbed his wrist with the other hand and tried to squeeze the pain away, but just as suddenly as it had arrived, it disappeared. He spent a few seconds trying to work out what had happened, his head still spinning. He grabbed his bag, stuffed all his books back into it and slowly got to his feet. He was left with the oddest sensation that Evi would not be waiting with Tina for the walk home.

Art waited at the school gates for Walt, who eventually ran out waving his homework.

'I got an A! Another one!'

'Hey that's great, little bro,' Art praised, still holding his wrist. 'Did that photo of the world from space help? You know that was taken during the very first complete orbit of the planet.'

They headed off down the road.

'Yeah, I know!' Walt enthused. 'Thanks for getting it for me. You didn't have to do that.'

'I know, but I wanted it to be good for you,' Art said.

'You nearly didn't get yours finished, did you?' said Walt.

'Oh, I got it in on time,' lied Art.

'Oh yeah, how did you do with your homework?' asked Walt, and immediately wished he hadn't when Art looked uneasy.

Quick as a flash, Walt got a plastic box out of his bag and opened it.

'Here, have a cookie – we made these today. They've got white chocolate in them.'

50

Art took one and bit into it.

'Hey, not bad, little B. Oh, we're coming up to Grandma's house. Wanna pop in with me?'

Walt looked puzzled about something. 'I thought we were walking home with Evi Wise today?' As usual, Walt didn't miss a trick.

'Yeah, so did I,' said Art. He had had a feeling Evi wouldn't be at the school gates with Tina, but hadn't suspected that *neither* would be there. 'Are you coming in or not?' he asked.

'Okay,' Walt said. 'This time I'm gonna beat her, though. And I'm having the wireless controller, okay?'

'You got it, Walt.'

Art lifted the latch on the gate and they both walked through into the explosion of colour that was Grandma's front garden. The grass looked as though it had been painted green, all the flowers were in full bloom and the rows of vegetables in the far corner were thick with leaves and shoots, ready to be harvested. They walked up to the bright red front door and Art pushed the old-fashioned doorbell button right in the middle. There was a shuffling of feet that grew louder and louder, and the door opened. Grandma Elfee stood dressed in what looked like a blue boiler suit, holding a trowel in one hand and the wireless controller for the computer games console in the other. Her long white hair was tied back in a ponytail as usual.

'Ah, boys! Come in, come in, dears. I was just doing a spot of gardening, so I was. I'll get a pot of tea on,' she said in her soft Irish accent.

Art had always wondered how she managed to keep her clothes so spotlessly clean while gardening. Even the trowel she was holding was immaculate, the metal still smooth and shiny like it had never been used.

Walt ran up to her and hugged her briefly before reaching for the controller and disappearing into the living room. She smiled after him, then turned towards the kitchen, motioning for Art to follow. She put a saucepan of water on to boil, and they both sat down at the table. Art smiled at the old-fashioned way she insisted on making tea.

51

'Did you like the cake this morning, Art?' she said.

Art still had the taste of Walt's cookie in his mouth, but it was hard to forget Grandma Elfee's cooking.

'Awesome, thanks, Gran. Have you got any more?' Art replied.

'Well, I shouldn't really,' she said, as she crossed the kitchen and retrieved a large plastic tub from a cupboard. She opened it and put it on the table.

Art reached in and grabbed a chunk of cake and bit into it. The smell and the taste were almost explosive, but at the same time calming and relaxing.

'Your cakes are brilliant!' he said, breathing through his nose.

She smiled fondly and took a piece for herself.

'I had an amazing teacher. Heart of gold, that man. Such a shame…' Her eyes glazed over and she got up to make the tea from the now boiling pan of water.

Quick as a flash, Walt ran in, snatched a piece of cake and ran out, saying, 'ThanksGrannicecake.'

He was in and out in less than two seconds, and Grandma continued making the tea.

'Do you have the tub I gave you the cake in this morning, dear?' she asked over her shoulder.

'Oh yeah…' Art replied, and unzipped his bag to rummage around for it at the bottom. As he did so, his little notebook fell out and landed open at the page he had doodled on.

Grandma turned to take the box from him and noticed the book on the floor. Her eyes widened and she gasped in shock.

'That's it…' she said, 'you've finished it…' She picked it up and asked Art if she could have a look.

'Oh that,' he said – then he remembered the shock he had had that morning. He gasped and quickly found the box, whipped out the note and unfolded it. The insignia was exactly the same as in his notebook, but before he could say anything, Grandma had snatched it out of his hand and was studying the two together, mumbling as she did so.

'That's it … it's finished … it's completely finished. That means it must be…' She stood up and placed them both on the table, staring into space. She grasped her wrist absent-mindedly. 'But I don't … it's too soon, surely…' Then her face visibly relaxed and she smiled warmly. 'Of course … New Year,' she whispered. Still looking into space, she said 'How's your arm feeling now?'

Art couldn't believe what he was hearing.

'Whoa! How did you...?' Art stared at her with wide eyes. How had she known about the incident in the corridor?

She smiled at him warmly.

'I know more than you think, Arthur, and it's nearly time for you to know some more too, so it is.' She narrowed her eyes. 'But not quite yet,' she added.

Art rubbed his wrist, and watched while his grandma walked over to a cupboard and opened it. Tucked neatly down beside a stack of plates was a brown parcel tied with hairy string. She removed it carefully and sat down across from Art at the table. She handed it to him, saying nothing. He held it carefully; it looked very old and fragile.

'What's this?' Art said.

'Open it and see,' she replied.

Art turned it over and untied the string, then carefully removed the stiff dusty paper. He was looking at the back of a framed picture; he turned it round. It was an intricate painting of a country scene, focusing on a small wooden hut in the middle resting on a slight hill. It had a small door, and a window on each side. The end wall was built of large stones that rose up to form a simple chimney, from which smoke was rising up into the sky. Although this gave it a homely feel, the hut looked way too small to be a residence of any kind. It looked old, but nonetheless very sturdy. The hill it was resting on was unnaturally green, and the sky was unnaturally blue, and that was when Art noticed something odd. There was a bright red sun, but next to it was what looked like a small red moon. It was a deeper red than the sun, and was covered in craters painted with incredible detail. There were some trees next to the hut, and the detail of the shadows on the ground of the sun shining through the leaves made it look like a photograph; Art had to stare closely to see that it really was a painting. The frame was crafted in wood, smooth and plain, but the finish was comparable to Art's own skill. It was even made from one piece of wood rather than four pieces connected together, just as he thought a frame should be. The whole thing looked priceless, and he was in awe of the skill that had gone into it. He spoke at last.

'Wow, Gran, it's err, well it's amazing!'

'I've been there,' she said. 'It's the most amazing place you will ever know, with more power than you can imagine. And it's waiting for you, Art, right now.' She was looking at him to see how he would react.

He said simply, 'Where is it?'

Grandma Elfee smiled more warmly than Art had ever seen her do before.

'It's my home,' she said, 'and soon it will be yours.'

'What do you mean by that?' said Art.

'Oh, well let's see. Think now, is there anything unusual in your life, Art? Anything at all?'

His mind started racing around Maga and Cinny, and how unusual the last four Christmases had been. One of the most unusual things, now that he thought about it, was how ordinary they had seemed. But how could Grandma Elfee possibly know anything about that? Maga's existence had been a closely guarded secret, known only to himself, and in a small way to Dr Levvy. Art looked into her eyes and knew she was seeing right through him.

She sat back in her chair. 'I thought so,' she said. 'So tell me this, has the Fragment found you yet?'

54

And straight away Art made the connection. His doodles, the insignia on Grandma's letter and the amulet in the small box with the unusual ribbon sitting in his bedside drawer at home. This was what she meant.

'Why do you call it that?' he asked.

Grandma Elfee's eyes lit up. 'It has! Oh that's so wonderful, Art – you must show me it, right away … no, no, I'm getting ahead of myself.' She leaned forward again. 'Where is it?' she asked.

'It's at home. I found it during the Christmas holidays in a little box, wrapped up in this strange ribbon that just … well it just…'

'I know,' she said, 'I can just remember how it happened before.'

Art was taken aback by this.

'What do you mean, how it happened before?'

'Well, I wasn't actually there, but he was pretty clear. They both were actually…'

'Gran!' Art shouted. He stood up and let the picture fall to the table. 'None of this is making any sense! This whole week has been ... just ... wacky and weird. And now you, and ... WHAT IS GOING ON?'

Grandma Elfee was not fazed in the slightest by Art's outburst, and she stood up. It was only now that Art noticed how agile she was, how quickly she had snatched her note out of his hand and how easily she had forced the chair backwards towards the dresser. She seemed to be a completely different woman since she had spied the drawings in his notebook, and now her stance was energetic, her expression wild but warm.

'I can't tell you,' she said, 'but I know who you can ask.'

'Who?' Art demanded.

Grandma Elfee smiled again.

'Your friend in the little black car.'

Art froze. He knew who she was talking about, but it felt odd actually saying his name.

'M ... Maga?' he managed to say.

In a hushed voice, she said, 'This is the beginning of something very big for you, Art. It's been a long time coming, so it has, but you must grasp it with both hands. Do you hear me? Look at the picture.'

Art didn't move. She snatched it up and thrust it into his hands.

'LOOK at it!' she shouted. 'When the time comes, you must know what to do, Art. You must KNOW! Study this, learn every detail in every brushstroke. Concentrate on the detail, Art.'

Art stared at her incredulously. Had he not met Maga those four years ago he would have thought she was going mad, and this connection was the only thing stopping him from storming out of the house there and then. Instead, he stayed rooted to the spot, unable to decide what to do. They stood staring at each other for what seemed like an eternity. Grandma Elfee eventually walked back over to the stove and finished making the tea, only this time he noticed she used two different powders from little pots, one black, the other a light brown. It smelled a little like tea and coffee mixed together when she added the boiling water and poured it into two cups. She added a drop of milk and half a spoonful of honey to each and brought them back to the table. She sat down, and Art did the same for want of something better to do. She sipped her drink, closing her eyes in bliss.

'I've waited so long for the moment when I could brew this again, so I have. Now that you're so close, it won't matter if you know.' She pushed his cup towards him. 'Try it.'

Art looked at his cup with an odd expression.

Grandma Elfee rolled her eyes. 'Don't tell me you've never smelled this before. If I know Maga like I think I do, he'll have brewed this right in front of your very eyes.'

Art couldn't argue with that, although Maga's methods of boiling water were somewhat more unusual and he hadn't bothered with milk or honey; Art had to admit that Grandma's smelled much better. He tried it. It was good. It had the strength and bite of coffee, and the aroma of tea when he breathed out through his nose. The whole experience was warming and calming. They sat there in silence finishing their hot drinks, with Art staring at the picture and Grandma Elfee staring at Art knowingly.

After a while, she took his cup and stood up. 'It's time now,' she said; 'take the picture and walk home. Go the long way. Think some.' She picked up his notebook and handed it to him. 'And this time, trust the Fragment. You're ready now.'

Art headed for the door.

'Don't worry about Walt, I'll feed him and drop him home once I've beaten him on the console so I will!'

And with that, Art walked out of the front door with his bag slung over his shoulder and the picture held tightly in his hand.

Back in the kitchen, Grandma Elfee stood at the sink washing the two cups, staring at nothing in particular.

'It won't happen as you think it will,' said a strong commanding voice.

'Oh shut up! This is it, I know it is,' she replied.

'No, this is the gap you are unaware of. The archives are very specific. This is the first time he goes, and it's not the same as you remember. Don't get your hopes up yet.'

'Either way,' she replied, 'it won't be long. I'll know as soon as I see his face tomorrow, so I will. Now shut up and load the game.'

Back in his room, Art whipped out his mobile phone and sent a text to Tina: *Strange things happening. Get over here quick.* Then he reached into his bedside drawer for the little box with the Fragment inside. The ribbon was lying next to it, but Art left that where it was. He opened the box, and this time the Fragment looked strangely familiar, like he had owned it all his life and had just discovered it again after years of being lost in the back of a drawer. The twine it was threaded onto looked smaller than it had at Christmas, and Art wondered if it would still fit around his neck. He looked closely at the Fragment. It was beautifully crafted, and glinted in multicolour when it caught the light. The silver it was crafted from was shining like new, but it had the air of an old antique, perfectly preserved. *This time, trust the Fragment,* Grandma had said. Trust it with what? Or to do what? Art had no idea. Then, without realising it, he started wrapping the twine around his wrist. He paused, slightly surprised, but then continued. *Trust the Fragment,* he thought. He wrapped it round and round, and threaded the last loop in on itself, with the Fragment resting on his wrist like a watch. Then it started pulsing, and the contours of the carvings started glowing. Art could feel the Fragment beginning to warm in his hands and he thought it might burn him. He tried to take it off, but Grandma Elfee's words kept playing in his mind, so he relaxed and let it happen, albeit reluctantly. It warmed to a comfortable level, but no more.

His mind began to wander of its own accord. He thought of Walt, and how he had helped him over and over again with his homework at the expense of his own. He thought of Peter, and how he had walked up to him on his first day to see why he was crying. He thought of Tina, and how he had been friends with her for so long. He thought of Dr Levvy, and how she had helped him every year at the hospital. He thought of Maga and Cinny, and the laughs they had had together over the years. And lastly he thought of Evi. Nothing specific, just an image of her, blurring his senses. Then his attention snapped back into focus. What had just happened? It had felt like an invasion of his memories and he didn't like it. But suddenly he didn't care so much. A great fatigue was washing over him, and although he still felt in control, he had an irresistible urge to lie down and let the day end right there. He sat on the edge of his bed and swung his legs up. And just as his senses started deserting him, the door to his room opened and he could just make out a blurry image of Tina standing over him, her eyes wide with shock. But he didn't care about that either. Blissful sleep swept through him, and everything went black.

'Jimma – activity in the portal. Processing. Single traveller, no vehicle. No clearance, no pass even, no ID, no destination available. He's locked in stasis. Want a look?'

'No pass? Are you sure? Nothing at all?'

'Zip. Hang on, there's more trickling through. Male. Fifteen years old, just a youngster. The full schematic's come up.'

'We can't see anything just from that, Pud. Give me full colour. I want a picture of this one.'

'Okay, give me a sec ... he's in an awkward position. Let me just shift him a bit so we'll see him more clearly. That's better. Right, bringing up the palette. You want everything, Jimma?'

'Everything. Full colour.'

'Coming up. Ah, he must have come from somewhere dark, as there's no light coming off him at all. Just a black picture.'

'Well, it's a start.'

'No, I can do much better than that. This new console can add light to a subject even in stasis. I'll have to move him on a few nanoseconds though. Are you sure you want to do this?'

'Yes, I'm sure. It looks like he's asleep anyway. He won't notice a thing.'

'Okay. Sliding, illuminating, and ... stopped. Bingo! Full colour.'

'Well, well, well, what do we have here? Infant human, dressed in sleeping clothes. No shoes, no hat. Looks fairly innocent to me. Pud, I don't suppose you noticed what was wrong with this picture when it first came up, did you?'

'I had a feeling. He's asleep. He can't have put himself through. Somebody must have done it for him.'

'Spot on, Pud. We need help on this one. Let's get all we can first, though. Do a DNA analysis to see if he's on any of the pass lists.'

'Okay. I'll have to roll him on another few nanoseconds, though; getting a cell sample needs real-time. You sure?'

'Got any better ideas?'

'Okay, okay. Sliding, sampling ... and ... stopped. Got it. Analysing. Wow! Computer's surprisingly quick with this one. The file's come up already. Ah. Four-Star Clearance only. Password required. That's odd. What's the password?'

'I don't think so, Pud. Step aside please.'

'Oh don't be so up yourself. Give me the password.'

'Do I have to pull rank on you, Pud? As the holder of Four Gold Stars you know I'm...'

'Sor-ry. Do excuse me, oh exulted one. The console is yours. Do you know how to work it?'

'Very funny, Pud. My uncle designed it, remember?'

'How could I forget? Is that how you got your fourth star so qui...'

'PUD!'

'Okay, okay, keep your hat on.'

'Thank you. Could you turn around, please?'

'Oh, what?'

'I have to type in the secret password.'

'That is the stupidest thing I ever heard.'

'One more instant of insubordination and I'll have you up in front of the board. DO I MAKE MYSELF CLEAR?'

'Crystal. Turning around in my chair. Turning around almost complete. Turning around complete. Secret password typing accessible.'

'Pud, I'm warning you. Right. In it goes, printing, and ... deleted. You can turn back now. And no more of your lip. Got it?'

'Okay. What does it say, Jimma? What does it say? Come on, who is he? Jimma, are you okay? Jimma?'

60

'Oh, my. Err, wow! Pud, could you rotate him slowly so we can see his right arm?'

'What for?'

'Just do it, will you?'

'Okay. Horizontal axis alright? Turning. There it is. Th ... oh my ... is that the ... what is he doing with ... so he's...'

'Exactly.'

'Oh my, Jimma. What do we do?'

'You do exactly as I tell you, okay?'

'Okay.'

'Good. Patch me a line directly through to the Boss. Don't go through anyone. ANYONE. Got it?'

'But that takes a Uniform Red Connection request.'

'Well done, Pud. So what are you waiting for?'

'Patching. Will my access codes do?'

'For this they will. Get on with it.'

'Coming online, Connection requested ... accepted! That was quick! Bringing up the speaker.'

'No, give me the headset, Pud.'

'Okay, you're a go.'

'Yes, hello, sir. How was the collection this year? Successful as ever I hope? Did you reach the quota? Well done, sir! Err, we, err, have a situation down here, sir. Well, it's him, sir. He's come through. Yes, I was as surprised as you are, sir, but the DNA sample brought up his clearance and it ... err ... it says it was authorised by yourself, sir. That's right, sir. What shall I do? Well, he's wearing sleeping clothes, sir, like the kind you sometimes have to get for the older ones, you know the ones I mean? That's right, and no shoes or hat, none at all. And he's on his own, sir. No one with him at all, and I'm 99 per cent sure he didn't send himself through, sir. Someone did it for him. Well he's asleep, so he can't have. That's right. What shall I do? Yes, yes, yes, oh right. A what? But he's only fifteen, sir.

61

Are you sure? Okay, yes, yes, right away – consider it done, sir. Yes? Why, thank you, sir! I will, sir. And the same to you, sir. Thank you, goodbye!'

'Connection closed. What did he say, Jimma?'

'You'll find out soon enough. We need to kit him out right away. He's inappropriately dressed. Can you still use the palette while we do this?'

'Of course. What do you need?'

'Artisan's tunic, please.'

'What colour?'

'As plain as possible. Light brown; is that easy?'

'As easy as it gets. Over the top?'

'No, replace them with what he's wearing. That's good. Now, some decent travelling boots. Leather, supple, wound up to his knees. Nice and snug.'

'There you go. What next?'

'Leather sheath, for his Sta'an.'

'For a fifteen year old?'

'Just do it, will you?'

'Okay. Open ended or encasing?'

'Open ended. Good work.'

'What kind of hat, Jimma?'

'No hat, Pud.'

'What? No hat? Whatever do you mean?'

'I mean, no hat. It means without a hat.'

'Okay, you're the boss.'

'Now, unpatch the palette and the whole schematic, and set him down at these coordinates.'

'Okay, resuming linear movement at one quarter. He's through. Are we just supposed to leave him like that? With no protection?'

'Apparently, he doesn't need it. He'll be fine, I have the Boss's personal assurance.'

'My, oh my! Alone in Scem's district with no hat. I'll be a console designer's nephew.'

'No, that's me, Pud. Stroth brew if you please. I could do with one.'

'Can't we monitor him just for a bit?'

'Two drops of honey, Pud.'

'But, Jimma...'

'Dough drops, Pud, don't forget the dough drops.'

Chapter Six

The L-Shaped Village

Never before had Art slept so badly. He tossed and turned, unable to get comfortable; he could not remember his bed having ever felt so rough and hard. Whenever he tried to pull the duvet over himself, it seemed to leave little bits of itself down his pyjama top. Nevertheless, Art's body was racked with fatigue, so he ignored the funny behavior of the duvet. He remembered he had drawn the curtains before getting into bed, so why was there so much light? And he definitely remembered putting out the snarling kitten, so how did it get back in?

The snarling kitten? Art shot into an upright position and was suddenly confronted by a very small furry cat-like animal with pointed ears and funny hand-like paws. It was snarling loudly in a high-pitched growl and scraping at the ground with its twenty little fingers. It was soon joined by two slightly larger animals, one a lighter brown, the other a little lighter still. Both were growling in support of their companion.

Art scrambled back in horror. He was sure they would follow him, but they stood their ground, snarling and scraping, making no effort to pursue him. When he was far enough away, they lost interest and wandered off, throwing back the occasional scowl and snarl.

Art surveyed his surroundings – this was definitely *not* his room. He was in a very large wood, with a heavy carpet of leaves and bark. He seemed to be covered in the stuff - he must have pulled it all over himself in the night. It certainly felt as if he had - there were reams of the stuff up his top and bottoms. He reached in and pulled it all out, watching it blend into the floor as it landed where it had come from.

And he was no longer wearing his school uniform either, but a rather tight-

64

fitting but flexible top in a fine light-brown cloth and similar trousers in a darker material. His shoes were made from a rough-looking but surprisingly supple leather, each with a single long strap wound round his ankle that reached almost up to his knees and tied neatly to hold them in place. Around his waist he had a newly made empty sheath, minus a weapon. His watch was gone, but the amulet was still there, secure as ever.

Art was very confused. He knew what dreaming felt like, and he was sure that he wasn't dreaming right now. So how had he ended up here? He looked around. Trees were visible in every direction, stretching far into the distance with seemingly no end. He widened his eyes in an attempt to see more clearly in the gloomy light, and eventually his gaze rested on a faint but definite path that led into the trees. With no idea where he was, but nowhere else to go, Art decided to follow it. Fully awake now, he walked quickly, his alert senses forcing him to look from left to right as he went.

Before long, the trees began to disperse as he neared the edge of the wood, and Art could make out an unusually blue sky. He soon emerged onto a stretch of bright green grass running over hills and valleys, bathed in brilliant sunshine. To his left was a great expanse of water, a lake shining a brilliant blue, with fish jumping in and out and splashing back down like there was nothing more wonderful to do. Little boats were tied up along several wooden piers, the first sign of civilisation since his arrival. The scene on his right, however, made his heart skip a beat.

It was the exact same scene from the painting he had seen in his grandma's house. The grass led up a slight hill, perched on the top of which was the small hut with the two windows and the stone chimney. In the picture, smoke was pouring from the chimney, but there were no such signs of life here. In the sky to the left of the chimney was the bright red sun, which dwarfed the little luminescent red moon just below it and off to the right. Its surreal red shine was far more mystical than Art remembered from the painting, but then Art supposed no paint could ever be that colour. He was strangely drawn to the little hut and walked closer.

65

Art stood facing a rather stern-looking wooden door and turned the brass handle with little effort. As the door creaked open, a huge cloud of dust engulfed him. He fanned it away and peered inside. There was very little to see inside the hut apart from a small wooden table and two chairs, and a solid brick fireplace with a black grate. There were the old remains of a fire, suggesting it had not been used for a long time. Along all of the walls were rows of hooks, some empty, others holding furry coats and hats in neutral colours of brown or black and made from a finely weaved material that Art didn't recognise, all superbly lined and stitched. The hut smelled of his grandma's house.

Art was still very tired, and as this familiar little hut was the closest he had felt to home in a while, he ventured inside and sat down heavily in one of the chairs, listening as it creaked and groaned under his weight. But he immediately jumped back up when he saw what was beyond the window. The most beautiful little valley stretched down for a mile or two like a little bowl, completely covered in a thick blanket of snow, with more falling thick and fast from the white sky. Art looked out of the opposite window, by the wooden door, and saw the sunny, green and blue landscape he had come from, but unquestionably, the other side of the hut was as snowy as a winter could get.

He ran back outside in disbelief, around the side of the hut, and faced the snowy valley. The snow started about five or ten yards away from the hut, but before this the grass was as green as everywhere else. As Art continued to stare at the valley, the snow gradually stopped falling. He squinted as visibility slowly improved, and in the distance he could just make out a faint collection of lights, suggesting a settlement of some kind.

For the first time since he had woken up in this strange place, the amulet showed signs of life. It clicked twice as if trying to get his attention, and then gently lifted Art's arm by the wrist. Art looked down at the amulet and then back to the valley. There was no doubt that the amulet was trying to lead him, but as he was about to step out into the snow a thought crossed his mind. As lovely as it looked, Art was sure he would freeze to death if he walked into the snow in such simple clothes. The settlement was easily a five-minute walk away, and the thick blanket of snow was proof that there were some serious minus temperatures at work. Looking anything but new, his clothes were comfortable and practical but certainly not built for such cold weather. So what was the amulet doing?

The amulet clicked twice again, as if it had read Art's thoughts, and started to emit a reddish orange glow. As Art stared at it in wonder, he could feel warmth coming from it, which travelled slowly up his arm, past his shoulders and into the very core of his body. Every inch of him was now toasty warm, and he thought he might melt the snow the moment he walked on it.

Again, the amulet tugged at his arm.

'Okay, okay,' he said, 'I get the message.'

He stepped gingerly into the snow. The air was completely different and instantly much colder, and the wind that blew smelt like the first bitter winds at the end of autumn. The cold whipped around Art's body, but the amulet was keeping him completely immune. He stared at it as it glowed steadily on his wrist as he walked, and wondered for the umpteenth time where on earth it could have come from and why he had it.

As he neared the settlement, it grew steadily clearer through the falling snow. It became apparent that it resembled a small village, comprising a dozen or so small houses arranged in an L-shape. The roof of each house was covered in snow, and each chimney was smoking, with a warm glow coming from every snow-covered window. Along the longest stretch of the L-shape, a string of streetlights illuminated the surrounding area with small flickering flames. It looked like a little high street, and was the most cosy-looking, welcoming little village Art had ever seen.

As he moved closer, he could see that some of the houses were actually shops, and had large snow topped signs with red writing on them. There was a food and hardware shop, a furniture shop, a shop with a sign Art couldn't read yet, two cafés and an inn called The Horn Keeper, but the biggest shop of all was called The L-Shaped Village Meeting Hall.

Just at that moment, a horse and cart exited the side entrance of one of the houses. Initially, Art thought nothing of it, but then he noticed that the 'horse' was like nothing he had ever seen before. It was much hairier for a start, and he was sure that horses were supposed to only have four legs, not five. The fifth leg was muscular and central, and swung in front of the animal like an elephant's trunk, obviously not intended to help it to walk. It had a large hand-like hairy foot on the end, slightly bigger than the other four feet, and occasionally kicked things out of the way - old wooden crates, bits of rubbish, worn out barrows. The cart was also rather peculiar. It resembled a sleigh with skis, but had big wheels hooked onto the sides. Art could see where the axle fittings would be fixed to replace the skis. The driver was a thin little man with a thick coat and a pointed red hat; Art couldn't quite see his face. The cart disappeared around the corner just as another face appeared through one of the windows to the inn.

As Art ventured forward he could see that it was a slim little face with bright blue eyes and a pointy chin. He wore a pointed yellow hat with a red band around it, and his face was screwed up as he tried to see through the misted window. He raised a thin but robust-looking hand to wipe it clear, and as he did so, Art could see that the little man was talking to someone. Every so often his face would turn sideways to speak to them, but his eyes continued to scan the horizon. Then he caught sight of Art and the little man stopped mid sentence, his eyes wide. His jaw dropped and his hand spread itself against the window. He turned and shouted something rather hurriedly to whoever was with him, took one more look at Art by pressing his face against the window and then disappeared from view.

Art was less than a hundred yards from the village now, and little tugs from the amulet had made sure he was heading directly for the inn. Art could see that the roof of the inn had two chimneys smoking rather heavily, and a third that was covered in snow and like an upside-down cone shape.

Just then the muffled sound of a foghorn blasted from the third chimney. There was a pause, then air blasted from the cone and snow and dirt, as well as a few birds, flew out of the top. The snow fell away and Art could now see that it was a rather dirty brass horn, far larger than any he had seen before. The horn blew again, this time clear and loud – a long deafening bass note that shook the whole village and cleared some of the snow from the surrounding rooftops.

Faces appeared at the windows of all the houses, some stuffing on their hats as they wiped their windows clear; then doors flew open and the little road was suddenly filled with excited people - if you could call them people.

Some were small and thin, others rather portly with round bellies; the men with wrinkled faces and pointy chins, the women with slightly more rounded faces and far smoother complexions. They all had bright blue eyes, so bright that they almost shone, and everyone, even the children, was wearing a hat of some kind. Most wore pointy hats in various bright primary colours, but a few were more like bowler hats, black and dull. Those wearing the bowler hats were dressed in business-like black jackets with brightly coloured ties and shirts, rough black canvas trousers and smart black shoes with brightly coloured laces. The others were wearing roughly sewn tops and bottoms, remarkably similar to Art's, but very brightly coloured and remarkably clean. In their haste, they had forgotten to put on warm coats, and some were starting to shiver.

The doors to The Horn Keeper were the last to open. The little man from the window emerged and walked through the crowd, everyone making a point of stepping aside to let him through. Art could see a ring of dirt around his mouth – he must have been the hornblower. He wore a well-fitting coat of bright blue and red material, held together with large but very neat stitches. He wore dark trousers that were more like bandages wrapped neatly around his legs, and on his feet he wore robust walking boots, very ordinary apart from the bright-red patterned laces. His hat was sleek, bright yellow and shiny. It was very aerodynamic, like it had been swept back by the wind, and there was a symbol resembling a pair of crossed policeman's clubs stained in dark sap on one side.

Around his waist was a sheath exactly the same as the one Art was wearing, inside which sat a very ornate-looking weapon with a shiny heart-shaped ruby set into the handle. A very blunt protrusion, like a conical blade made of wood stuck out of the bottom of the sheath, on which some writing was neatly embossed onto it. The blade seemed to glow the colour of moonlight, and resembled an expensive futuristic baton. Art realised that this was probably what was depicted in the symbol on his hat.

'Hité!' the man shouted excitedly. 'It's happened, it's happened! Someone's come from the hut! Look! He doesn't wear a hat!'

The crowd to the left of the little man hurriedly moved aside and a very pretty woman appeared, slightly shorter than the little man, but with a definite air of confidence. She was wearing a cream-coloured jacket with burgundy baggy trousers and funny little boots with rather ordinary laces. She wore her bright white hair in a ponytail underneath a hat of a rather lighter shade of yellow than the little man's. The symbol on her hat showed a circle with a tree in the middle, a horizontal zigzag line going through its centre.

Art noticed that all the brightly coloured hats had symbols on them, but most were too far away for him to make out. However, one looked like a hammer or an anvil, and another an easel and paintbrush. A group of twenty or so slightly smaller people were also present and all dressed exactly the same, and Art could swear that they all wore hats with the same symbol as on the hornblower's hat, but he could not be sure.

The pretty woman took the man's hand and squeezed it reassuringly. She looked Art up and down. Art was now standing in the middle of a semicircle of strange and curious, but somehow welcoming people.

'Scem,' she whispered, 'did he really come out of the hut? I mean, he could be just anyone. You know how vague the Scriptures can be.'

Scem – apparently the little man – thought for a moment, and also looked Art up and down. His gaze fell upon the empty sheath around his waist and a small smile crossed his face. He looked behind Art and noticed the tracks he had made in the snow. Art could see his eyes following them to the hut in the distance, and then he fixed his gaze back on Art.

'Most definitely, my dear,' he said, not taking his eyes off Art. 'Just look at his tracks.'

The villagers wowed and aaahd at the brilliance of Scem's deductive powers, careful to quieten when they thought he wanted to continue.

'He appeared inside the hut, just like we thought he would … most of us anyway,' he said, emphasising the last part with the intention of making the others hear it. 'And he walked straight here. It's all just like the Sacred Horn said.'

Scem released Hité's hand and walked casually over to Art, stopping a few feet in front of him, with each foot firmly planted in front of the other as if in mid stride, his arms squarely at his sides. He waited … and waited.

Art looked round at the other villagers, hoping that something would happen, but they too were all staring at him expectantly. The pause was becoming a little awkward, and Art could see some of the villagers were growing restless. Even Scem's motionless expression was beginning to waiver. Art thought he should probably break the silence.

'Hello, err, I'm Art. I'm ever so sorry, but I have no idea where I am, and I was hoping you could tell me. I was in this wood with some very strange cat-type thingies, and then I found my way here, and then ... erm ... and ...'

The silence was *not* breaking as well as Art thought it would, and Scem's expression was beginning to take the shape of a frown. With a sudden look of realisation, Hité rushed forward and took Art's hand, shaking it politely.

'You meant to say how do you do, didn't you?' she said rather hurriedly. 'I am Hité. My husband Scem here is the warrior of the L-shaped Village.' She had a high-pitched but soft voice, with a slight lisp.

71

There was more silence, and a few strange winks from Hité. Art gave her a baffled look and opened his mouth to speak. Hité nodded frantically. *She must want me to introduce myself in the same way*, he thought.

'How do you do, I am Arthur,' he said, (more frantic nods from Hité), 'and I am, err, bottom of my class at most things.' In the rush to introduce himself in an appropriate manner, Art had said the first thing that came into his head, and he realised it was a surprisingly accurate account of his life.

Scem seemed to come back to life at these words, and he took Art's hand and shook it fiercely.

'Hello, err, R-Thor, Bottom Of Your Class At Most Things. I am Scem, Warrior of the L-Shaped Village. We've been expecting you, haven't we, Hité?'

Art could see some of the villagers looking at the ground sheepishly.

Scem moved closer and spoke in a low whisper. 'Well, most of us have. There are some who had doubts that you would come, but I … I mean *we*, had full confidence in you, R-Thor.' He moved backwards and spoke normally again.

'R-Thor, Bottom Of Your Class At Most Things, we have all today witnessed your coming from the hut, and wearing no hat. There is no doubt in my mind, as Warrior of the L-Shaped Village, that you are the one we have been waiting for. I think it is about time you came inside out of the cold.' He bent down on one knee. 'I would be honoured to make you a hot drink in my house, so that you can tell us your many stories and share your wisdom with…'

His eyes widened as he caught sight of the amulet wrapped around Art's wrist. He froze and slowly looked up, respect in his eyes.

'Wh…where did you get that?' he stammered.

Art looked down at it with a smile. It was still glowing, and he felt toasty warm.

'Oh that, well I suppose you could say *it* found *me.*' he said. 'It was a present from my grandma, and it seems to have taken a shine to me. It's been sort of looking after me since I got here. I can't really explain it.'

.Scem stood up and shouted back at his people.

'He's wearing the Fragment! The missing part of the Stone has returned, and R-Thor is its vehicle! Now do you believe the Scriptures?' *There's that word again,* Art thought – *the Fragment.*

There was an excited uproar, and even Hité stepped forward to inspect it. She looked up and smiled at him, then took Scem's hand once again. Scem turned back to Art. He was smiling broadly now.

'The Scriptures were true, R-Thor – this is a very exciting time. Any friend of the Fragment is a friend of mine. We have waited for its return for a long time indeed. It chose you as its passage back here, and soon its work will be done.' He placed his hand on Art's shoulder. 'You are welcome in my house as if it were your own, my friend.'

Scem put his arm around Art and led him towards The Horn Keeper.

'Stand aside, families. There will be plenty of time for you all to welcome our guest over the next few days.'

They all parted as hurriedly as before, and the air was full of excited whispers. Scem guided Art up the steps of the inn, which were deep in snow and crunched as they walked.

'I must admit though, R-Thor,' Scem said casually, 'for the greatest warrior there ever was I'm surprised to see you without your Sta'an.'

And with that they entered Scem and Hité's warm house, with an excited crowd of twenty or so villagers peering in through the windows.

Inside the warm and welcoming inn Hité pulled up three chairs, with one either side of Art, at a large, round, perfectly crafted wooden table. She sat down and waited for Scem to return from the kitchen. When he did so, he was carrying a saucepan full of a steaming brown liquid, which smelled of both tea and coffee. Art could hardly believe it. *That's Stroth-Brew – whatever that is,* he thought. Scem poured a mug for each of them.

73

Art found himself sitting in the large public area of the inn, which looked as if it doubled as Scem and Hité's front room. There were tables and chairs everywhere, all occupied by various members of the village, and a bar with large mugs all along its surface and bowls full to the brim with strange things that looked like nuts or dried fruit. The table they were sitting at was by the fire, as were two big old comfy chairs. The fireplace was a huge affair, constructed of massive stones cemented together, just like in the hut, to form the surround which filled most of the wall. Art thought the massive grate could probably hold a whole tree's worth of logs if it was fully stacked, which it wasn't.

Everything looked very quaint and antiquated, although to the right of the fireplace was a small metal square that looked like a light switch, with an emerald-coloured circle in the middle. Next to it was a line of lights the same size as the switch, flashing on and off in different patterns. They looked wildly out of place in this little inn, and Art wondered if there was more to this village than met the eye. On the walls were portraits of Scem and Hité in various poses, painted in bright colours and in carved wooden frames. Each of the paintings was signed 'Pedya' in an ornate scrawl at the bottom. They filled almost every inch of the walls, and with the flames from the fire flicking light around the room, Art could easily imagine this place full of loud, jolly people until the small hours of the morning.

Scem turned to face the rest of the villagers who had now entered the inn and were staring silently at Art, making him feel slightly uncomfortable. Only moments before, Scem had told them there would be plenty of time to 'welcome him properly during the week', whatever that meant, so he wondered why Scem had allowed them to trail in behind. He seemed to have pretty good authority over them.

A small but compact-looking man with a kind face was rushing about with a huge tray of jugs, filling all the villagers' mugs as quickly as he could. When he had finished, he emptied the tray of empty jugs, picked up the last remaining full one and threw away the tray, holding the jug up to

Scem as some sort of signal. Scem acknowledged him and stood up, allowing his chair to screech loudly as it was pushed backwards. Silence fell immediately.

Scem addressed the villagers in his best leader's voice, which sounded *nothing* like his normal voice. He kind of puffed out his chest and stood up a bit taller as he prepared to speak.

'My friends,' he announced, holding up his mug, 'for thousands of moonsets we have waited for the Warrior to arrive. And at last, out of the sun and into the snow, R-Thor has come, and in spectacular fashion I'm sure you'll agree.'

There were shouts of agreement from everybody present, and they banged on the tables with the palms of their hands. Again they were careful not to go on for too long.

'My darling wife kept the Scriptures on the Sacred Horn sparkling clean for years before we found each other, and relentlessly upheld the tradition right until the present day, a tradition that goes back thousands of years through the generations.' He inserted a functional pause. 'The words *were* truthful. Some of us *were* faithful. And now, we need be fearful no longer.' Another functional pause. He seemed very proud of this one.

he turned to Art. 'Welcome to the L-Shaped Village, R-Thor. You shall have everything you need this night until your own residence is ready. Drink up! And tell us of your adventures.'

And with that a great cheer erupted, followed by an immediate and startling silence as they all settled down very quietly to listen. It was an impressive silence. Scem's loud authoritative tone and the huge cheer from the villagers were a very good contrast to the total quiet, and seemed to actually emphasize it.

Art was at a total loss, this being the second awkward silence he had been confronted with. He didn't know what Scem was talking about; what adventures? And why did he keep calling him a warrior? Also, he was still rather confused as to where he was, how he had got there, what was in store

75

for him now he was here and, most importantly, how he could get back home. Was he supposed to stay here? And if so, for how long?

Just when the silence was becoming unbearable, Hité sighed loudly, rested her hand on Art's shoulder and spoke to him very quietly, too quietly for Scem to hear.

'It's okay,' she said, 'I understand. Please, just hold my hand and relax.' She took his hand and shifted her grip on it a few times until it rested with her palm directly over his. She closed her eyes and lowered her head.

Art looked at her with a puzzled expression, then turned his gaze towards the expectant villagers. He noticed that everything was becoming slightly blurred and he was beginning to feel lightheaded. His limbs felt very heavy and his eyelids felt as if they were weighted down. He very quickly lost the battle to stop them closing.

All of a sudden, he was aware of being in a dark room with a single occupant. The solitary figure was sitting on a small stool, and Art slowly realised it was himself. He saw that he was holding a large book, and reading it aloud. The words on the pages were blurred and misshapen, and he couldn't make them out. They slowly began to come into focus, but just when he thought he might be able to read what they said, he was sitting at the table again between Scem and Hité and in front of a silent audience. Surprisingly, he felt totally at ease, and even the silence no longer seemed quite so awkward.

'Art, drink your stroth brew,' Hité said softly, 'it'll warm you up.'

Art responded to the soothing voice as if hypnotised and took a sip from his mug, even though he wasn't the slightest bit cold.

Hité stood up and walked behind Art towards Scem, who was sitting comfortably in his chair ready to listen to Art's great tales of adventures and battles. She took Scem's hand and looked at him closely.

'Scem, my darling, we really need to be alone with him for a while. I told you he wouldn't know why he was here and I have just looked, he doesn't. Everybody must go at once.'

Scem gave her a look of total bewilderment and, for a moment, was speechless.

'What do you mean, he doesn't know?' he asked eventually. 'Everything the Scriptures said has come true, hasn't it? Everyone knows why he's here – he can't be the only one who doesn't. The idea's utterly preposterous!'

Hité put her arm around his shoulder. 'We've been through this before, haven't we? It's all about *interpretation*, Scem. The Scriptures can sometimes be vague to those with less than a completely open mind.'

'I understand that, my dear,' Scem continued, 'but look what's around his waist – he's a Warrior through and through, just like they said he would be.'

'He also wears the boots of a traveller and the clothes of an artisan. Not to mention his large craftsmen's hands,' Hité reasoned. 'Trust me, darling; I have never yet been wrong. Everyone must go. Please.'

Scem opened his mouth to protest, but Hité quickly put her hand on his cheek and looked at him lovingly. 'Darling, now please.'

He immediately closed his mouth, dropped his head and let out a huge sigh, looking grief-stricken. His tiny hand slapped the table and his leader's voice boomed.

'Everybody out, everybody out! Like I said, there will be plenty of time to welcome our guest over the coming week. But for the moment, he needs rest. Quickly now, everybody out.'

The villagers stood up sulkily and moaning sound rose among them. A few drained their tankards on the way out, and before long they were alone.

Scem bolted the doors while Hité led Art over to one of the large comfy-looking double chairs by the fire. Hité sank slowly into one of them and Scem joined her, having refilled the saucepan and placed three clean mugs on the small fireside table. His movements were particularly lethargic now. He filled the mugs and gave one to Art, another to Hité, and started sipping from his own rather absent-mindedly. They sat by the fire for a short while listening to the soft hissing and crackling, absorbing the heat.

77

Art was still euphoric from his unusual experience, and he was glad for the time to clear his head. The warm drink was reassuring enough, but quite sour. Art thought it would taste a lot better with a spoonful of sugar or two. Or maybe some honey. And a drop of milk. At last, the silence was broken, with Hité being the first to speak.

'R-Thor, I am sorry that had to happen to you. I never meant it to. My darling Scem is a little overexcited; I'm afraid you'll have to forgive him.'

The drinking of the Stroth-Brew was almost ceremonial, but Art saw that Scem was not really in the mood for contemplation. He was shifting restlessly. However, Hité seemed to have a knack of easing his hotheadedness before it boiled over, and she spoke again.

'Now, R-Thor, why don't you tell us, as slowly as you like, who you are and all about the Fragment you have on your wrist. There's no rush, and there's plenty more Stroth-Brew should you run out.'

There it was again - a reference to Stroth-Brew. Art supposed this Stroth-Brew must be more than just a hot drink, and sometimes used as an action to give time to mull over a problem or decision before discussing it with someone, like the good old cup of tea back home.

Art tried to clear his mind in order to make sense of the day's strange events, but the euphoria was clouding his thoughts. He thought long and hard, and eventually felt up to talking.

'My name,' he said gingerly, 'is Arthur, not R-Thor, but I like to be called Art. I'm fifteen years old and I'm a schoolboy, not a ... a *warrior*. I can't remember ever fighting anyone. I think this pendant thing brought me here, though I don't know how or why.' He chuckled. 'And I'm afraid I've never had any adventures.' He held up his mug. 'I don't suppose you have any milk and sugar, do you?'

Scem's mouth dropped open. He bashed his mug down on the table, spilling much of it, his face aghast.

'Fifteen years old? FIFTEEN?' He stood up. 'Fif... I would like to think that I still have a lot to learn in my station as the Village Warrior, and I'm in my sixty-fourth year! Fifteen?'

'I'm sorry,' Art said.

'But the Scriptures clearly say you're a Warrior,' Scem continued. 'You *are* a Warrior, aren't you? I mean, you're not anything *else*, are you?'

Art stared into his drink, hoping it would help him out of this hole.

'I don't really...'

'But that's impossible,' Scem continued. 'Your Sta'an won't find you for another ten years at least. It's just not possible.'

Scem was getting a little too worked up for Hité's liking now.

'But how can the Scriptures be wrong?' he added.

Hité took him by the hand and he visibly relaxed. He looked at her and slowly sat back down. She squeezed his hand and looked at him in that magical way of hers. He held his head in his hands, but at least he was quiet.

'The Scriptures say that he is the greatest Warrior that will ever live,' Hité began. 'They also say that he is the greatest Navigator, the greatest Mind-Charm, Artisan, Inspiration, Teacher, Student ... everybody reads it differently. Everybody who believes in the Scriptures thought he would be the greatest of their chosen paths, as that's what they read. And there was no telling them ... there was no telling *you*.'

Scem looked up at her.

'But he can't be all of them,' she continued. 'We will just have to wait and see what he is, as he clearly doesn't know *himself* yet.'

Scem was deflated. For so many years he had believed the Scriptures wholeheartedly, mostly out of devotion to Hité. Her mother had been the Horn Keeper when Scem had first wandered into the village accompanying his father on the yearly Collection Mission. During a well-needed lunch-time Stroth-Brew in The Horn Keeper Inn, the then young and vibrantly beautiful Hité had shown the Scriptures on the Sacred Horn to the young, headstrong Trainee Warrior, and he had never left since. Both sets of parents were

79

immediately overjoyed, the way it always was here.   Scem became the
Warrior of the L-Shaped Village, having trained so hard during the period
before their union that he surpassed the skills of others the village had seen
before, and Hité became the Keeper of the Horn shortly after. She ran the
inn, selling her own special brand of Stroth-Brew, and kept the Scriptures
and the Horn clean. Scem kept them all safe and ran the village with his
direct but compassionate approach to leadership, ensuring that it was the
Boss's centre for the Collection year in, year out. The Scriptures had become
part of his life, and he guarded them almost as ferociously as he did his wife.
His belief in their words made the Boss proud, and Hité even more so.

But the revelation that any part of the Scriptures could be wrong made
Scem feel uncertain of his own world. In his mind, there was no doubt that
the Scriptures said Art was a Warrior, the greatest there ever was, and he had
prepared himself throughout his whole adult life to learn from the great
leader the skills of perfect combat, flawless unquestioned leadership,
compassionate encouragement and moral judgment. But now it seemed there
was no such leader, no one to lead them through the impending wars
threatened by YerDichh if his demands were not met, threats that the Boss
was repeatedly ignoring, creating fear and uncertainty among even the
greatest of Warriors, including Emul of the LakeSide, Con'tek of the
Sunshine Valley and Jo'Sys of Trade Town. Scem of the L-Shaped Village
would be the last of the Fearless Warriors to lose his title of Fearless, and
this last blow seemed almost too much to bear.

Scem stared at the Sacred Horn and there was another long, awkward
silence. Hité gave Art a reassuring look, and then Scem slowly stood up,
squeezed Hité's hand affectionately and wandered outside into the snow,
letting the door slam behind him.

Art was beginning to feel uncertain again, and had it not been for the
comforting sounds of the crackling fire, the hot drink in his hands and the
company of this mysterious but friendly woman, he would have panicked at
this sudden surge of reality. But he kept his cool. Just.

He placed his drink down on the fireside table and calmly turned to Hité. He had never been more direct in his life, and he was sure the Fragment had something to do with it.

'I think, as a matter of courtesy,' he began, 'that I deserve to know where I am, who you and your people are and how I got here. And, perhaps most importantly, who you all think I am supposed to be, other than Arthur Elfee.'

Hité's eyebrows rose slightly at the name Elfee, but not enough for Art to notice. She was surprised by the calmness of his voice, and she put her mug down and turned to face him in a reassuring manner.

'Of course you do,' she said. 'I will tell you as much as I can, but I'm afraid there are parts you will have to wait for.' She stood up and began stoking the fire. 'In terms of who you are,' she continued, 'I'm afraid only you can tell us that, and as you don't know yourself, I can only assume that you are not the answer to our problems. At least not *yet*.' Hité knew this was not entirely true; his last name had confirmed it.

'As to *where* you are,' she smiled warmly and looked into the fire, 'I'm afraid I can't tell you that either.'

Art was a little disconcerted to hear this.

'I think I deserve to know that at least, Hité,' he insisted. It was the first time Art had used her name, and it brought the flicker of a smile to her face.

'I'm sorry, but I really can't tell you. I wish I could, but it's something you have to work out for yourself. Your heart is more than big enough, that much I have seen. It is better that it is slowly revealed to you over the next few days, or maybe months. I can only tell you *about* it.'

Hité couldn't help feeling sorry for him in this strange place and wished she could tell him more. But she knew that making the connections for himself was essential if he were to gain the right kind of thinking and stand a chance of making any difference here. She did feel, however, that she could let one thing slip, just to try and hurry things along a little.

'I know who you *can* ask, though,' she said.

Art looked up. 'Who?'

81

'Your friend in the little black car.'

Chapter Seven
Amarly

The next day, Art woke early in a large, comfy bed. The bedroom he had
been given was elaborately decorated, with scenes of vast landscapes painted
intricately on the walls and the ceiling a rich sky-blue, and chairs with
delicately embroidered cushions. The headboard was carved with strange
patterns that looked like the doodles he did at school, only much, much
bigger. He sat up with a start as he remembered the weird happenings of the
day before.

After the shock of the previous night and much protesting when Hité
refused to tell him how she knew Maga, she had suggested that he go to bed,
and it was only then that he realised how tired he was. He had been surprised
how quickly it got so late, and he suspected that the quiet period sitting by
the fire once the whole village had been ushered out of The Horn Keeper had
lasted rather longer than he had thought. His head had, after all, been in an
unusual state after the strange trick Hité had played on him that day, and
maybe time had flowed by rather more quickly than it had seemed to. He
had gone to bed willingly, though, feeling drained and confused, and longing
for the release of sleep.

This morning, however, he was much more alert, and was brimming with
questions. He threw off the covers and ran to the door, wrenching it open
and belting out of the room, throwing his top on as he raced down the
creaking stairs. He burst through the kitchen door and saw that Hité was
already there, preparing some of that strange drink again. But there were also
smells of cooking meat and toasting bread. Hité was calmly stirring a
saucepan of scrambled eggs, and the frying pan next to it contained sausages
and bacon, sizzling and popping.

Art was taken aback by all of this, as everything else he had seen since his arrival was peculiar. The standard of living seemed to be very basic and simple, and a full English breakfast looked strangely out of place. However, on closer inspection, he could see that the bacon was slightly burnt, the sausages were almost oblong in shape and there were three pieces of burnt toast still smoking in the bin, which he supposed had been Hité's first attempt. It was as if someone had told her what humans liked to eat for breakfast and she was trying to oblige.

'Morning, sleepyhead,' she said in a soft voice. 'Are you hungry? Breakfast's nearly ready. This is a great delicacy where you come from apparently – it's called a *flinglish*.'

She spoke to him as if seeing him in her kitchen was nothing out of the ordinary at all, and Art felt like a guest at a bed and breakfast.

'Well yes, I am actually,' he replied, 'but I need some questions answered first.'

Hité continued to stir the eggs calmly.

'I told you last night,' she said, 'it's best that you discover everything for yourself. Now sit down; you have a big day ahead and you'll need a big breakfast.'

'What do you mean, a big day?' he asked.

At that moment, Scem came through the door, walked up to Hité and kissed her on the lips, and then turned to face Art, rubbing his hands together.

'It's ready, all ready,' he said. 'We'll start when you've had your breakfast, R-Thor.'

Hité elbowed him in the ribs.

'Sorry, I mean *Art*,' he corrected himself. 'I don't suppose you have much luggage, but no doubt Jo'Sys of Trade Town will take care of that. Just come outside when you're ready, my friend.' And with that, he swept outside.

Art was puzzled by Scem's words.

'What does he mean, it's ready? What's ready?' he asked.

Hité reached into the pocket of her gown and brought out an exact replica of the very first model house Art had carved out of wood. It was a modest two-storey cottage with dark wooden rafters and glowing windows. She placed it on the table in front of him.

'Your house, of course. We have to move you into your new house.'

Art looked at the little carving, astounded. There was no doubt about it; he had carved this model during his first year of school. It had taken him little more than half an hour with all the wonderful new tools he had discovered in his father's shed, and he had lost it just as quickly. He had been furious, but had immediately set about carving another, far more basic one. He remembered how carving the first one had been so easy, as he knew exactly what to carve and where, while he had had to think so much harder about the second, which ended up being a sombre-looking block of flats painted in grey and black. He hadn't understood how he had come to lose the little cottage so easily; he had placed it on his bed with so much pride and happiness, but when he came back a moment later it had gone. Now it seemed he knew exactly what had happened to it.

Hité admitted she knew his trusted friend Maga, and it seemed that Maga had known about him for much longer than he had thought.

'No, no, no, NO!' he shouted angrily. 'How *dare* you! My first cottage! My first carving! Who are you? Just WHAT IS HAPPENING HERE?' Art slumped into the nearest chair and rested his head on folded arms, totally bewildered and confused.

Hité looked stunned. She dropped the wooden spoon in the saucepan and rushed over to sit down next to him.

Art held his head in his hands and said quietly. 'This is all happening too quickly. I don't know where I am, but I know I'm not at home. And I want to be. You keep going on about Warriors and Scriptures and stuff, and I don't know what any of it means.' He looked up slowly, staring into space. 'I'm not moving from this spot until I get some answers.'

'Now listen, Art...' Hité began.

'I'M NOT MOVING!' Art stood up. 'Let's see you try and give me a house or whatever it is when I won't move from this spot! That doesn't even make sense! But let's see it then, come on!' he cried.

Hité appeared very surprised by this outburst and was silent for a moment; then she jumped up to take the burnt eggs and meat from the stove as smoke began to fill the room. She turned back round slowly, as if she had given in, and let out a huge sigh.

'Okay, Art, I'll tell you all I can. But we are under orders to keep certain things from you, so don't expect too much, okay?' She sat down after scraping the charred remains of food into the bin. 'What do you want to know?'

Art thought for a moment. He had so many questions floating around in his head that he didn't quite know which to ask first. He decided to pick them off at random until there were none left, and he sat down, feeling a little calmer.

'Okay,' he said; 'first, why does Scem think I'm a warrior?'

'For the same reason that I thought you might be a Mind-Charm,' she replied. 'I kind of knew you wouldn't be, of course, but I secretly wanted you to be.'

Art looked confused. Was that an answer? Was this how the conversation was going to be?

'Do you know what a Mind-Charm is, Art?' she continued, hardly moving her lips.

This confused Art; had she said those words aloud or had he just heard them in his head? Then she spoke again, this time with her mouth firmly closed.

'That's right, Art, I know what you are thinking. Best of all, I know what you are going to say and do even before you do.'

Art was totally bewildered by what was happening. He stood up, stumbled backwards and fell over his chair. His Stroth-Brew flew

86

everywhere and the chair shattered as he landed on it. Hité was totally unprepared for this and rushed to help him.

'Art, I'm so sorry, I had no idea it would ... oh dear!' she cried, helping him up. Both of them were wide-eyed and slightly shaky. 'Art, I won't do that again, I promise. Come and sit down.' She sat him down on her chair, picked up his mug and rushed over to the stove to refill it.

Art didn't know what had just happened and couldn't speak for a while. Nothing like this had ever happened to him before. His mind raced and he seemed to remember everything at once up to the point when she had so rudely intruded on his mind. He vaguely remembered having his mind read the day before, but somehow the experience had been relaxing, as if he hadn't been allowed to believe it was happening. Everything that had happened since he had woken up in the forest had followed a certain logic based on Art's wild imagination, except exactly *where* he was and *how* he had got here. He knew that the moon here was the same as in his favourite picture at Grandma's house and that the hut smelled the same, so he could still be dreaming. But surely the sensation of actually being awake was unmistakable, and this all seemed too detailed and ordered to be one of his dreams.

Hité pulled round the chair that Scem had been sitting on and sat down, trying to read his expression. She handed him the Stroth-Brew and Art composed himself, determined to get some answers.

'What are the Scriptures? Where are they? What do they say?' he asked.

Hité smiled, gazing into space. 'That,' she said, 'is the biggest mystery of all.' She stood up and walked over to the corner of the room next to the big fireplace, which now sat lifeless except for a strange warmth emanating from it. 'Come and see for yourself,' she said.

Art walked over to where she was standing in front of a large brass cone that bent up sharply and rose through the ceiling. It was supported by large wooden struts, and the mouthpiece was broad and dented. Art recognised it as the big horn that he had seen sticking out of the roof the day before. It

87

rose to at least ten feet tall before it disappeared out of the ceiling, growing to almost five feet wide at the top. Art wondered how Scem had managed to get such an impressive sound out of it being such a small man. About halfway down the horn was some strange writing that continued right down to the mouthpiece. It appeared to be a lot of old gobbledygook about palaces, warriors and strange creatures destined to destroy the land and its princesses and dragons all sorts of weird and totally unbelievable things. Art nearly laughed, but immediately thought better of it.

Hité pointed to a small paragraph right at the bottom. 'Read from here, Art. Tell me what it says.'

Art moved closer and read in his best bedtime story voice, 'On the ten-thousandth moonset before the First Great Battle, look towards the Sun and Snow Hut, and walking through the snow shall be the Great Unitor, and He shall show you the way. Listen to him with understanding on the first coming, and on the second coming, when he shall stay forever; he shall know his calling. Draw upon his knowledge then, and then alone.'

Hité looked at him strangely. 'Unitor? Did you say *Unitor*?' she said.

Art checked the word. 'Yes, it's there in brass and, err, brass. Look.' He pointed to it.

Hité put her hand on his shoulder. 'That's the mystery, Art. Everybody reads *that* word differently. Scem reads it as *Warrior*, I read it as *Mind-Charm*. You say it reads *Unitor*.'

Art looked at the word again and then thought very hard. 'So, are you a, a mind-thingy, mind-charm then? And is Scem a warrior? Everybody has a place? A calling?'

Hité sighed a long, heavy sigh. 'You really don't know why you're here, do you?'

She picked up a rag and started polishing the brass horn absent-mindedly. Eventually, she put it down and steered Art back to the table.

'Dear Art, you have so much to learn. Come and sit down, and finish your Stroth-Brew.'

Stroth-Brew, again. Art was slowly starting to associate it with relaxation, and was amazed that he actually wanted to finish his mug. He thought he would wait to ask more questions until they had finished. He walked over and took his mug, but instead of sitting at the table, he wandered over to one of the comfy chairs and slumped into it, enjoying the sinking feeling. He looked around the spacious room.

On the walls he saw hundreds of paintings of Scem and Hité, most painted in vibrant colours and usually of their wedding day. Of the ones that showed the red sun, the deeper red crescent of the moon behind it always seemed a lot bigger. A lot of the paintings showed Scem and Hité outside the hut that smelled like Grandma's house; he had guessed by now that this was the Sun and Snow Hut that the Scriptures on the Horn talked about. All the paintings were in carefully carved wooden frames, bearing the name Tes-Chet carved into a signature clearly at the bottom. They covered every inch of the walls, so that there was no room for anything else. The light from the windows seemed to illuminate them, and the whole room felt very cosy and welcoming.

Hité returned from the stove with two hunks of fresh bread and plonked them down on the little knee-high table between the two chairs. Art thanked her as he warmed his hands on his mug. He wasn't particularly cold, but it comforted him to grip the hot mug as he looked around.

'Do you like our portraits?' Hité asked before Art could speak. 'Pedya painted them all himself. He still has a few more to do for us.' She paused for a moment, gauging the look on Art's face. 'Pedya is a painter; an artist, really. That's his chosen path. Everybody has one, you see. From a very early age children here usually know what they are naturally good at.'

Art thought for a moment. He remembered how he was instantly good at working with wood.

'My husband is a Warrior,' she continued, 'and I am a Mind-Charm.'

Art looked at the paintings again and noticed that in every one Scem was carrying the same weapon in the leather sheath around his waist as he saw

89

him wearing when they first met, with the jewel-encrusted handle. Art stood up and walked over to examine some of them more closely. The detail was so good that he could make out the emblems on their hats; the crossed swords on Scem's and the tree and lightning on Hité's.

Hité saw the realisation in his eyes, picked up her hat and walked over to him. She handed him the hat and he took it, intrigued. It was made of thick leather, and clearly stamped on each side was the symbol. Now that Art could see it up close, he could see that it wasn't a tree at all, but something that looked like two halves of a *brain*, with a flash of lightning running through it.

'It's my Crest,' Hité said. 'We all have one.'

'What does Scem's crest depict?' Art asked.

'That's a little more complicated. I'll let him tell you that when he thinks the time is right.'

They both stared at the pictures, Art transfixed by the bright colours for what seemed like an age. He noticed that the small red moon was shown as being much larger in the paintings than it actually was. He thought for second that this was because they were paintings and so were bound to have irregularities, but as he studied them more closely he saw that everything else was perfectly in proportion. Nothing was the wrong size or shape, and the colours were seemingly perfect. Could it be that when the paintings were created the moon was actually a different size? It suddenly became apparent to him that he was very far away from home.

'Hité, where am I?' he asked quietly. 'Where is *here*?'

Hité's face lit up with a warm smile, and she closed her eyes and rested her head in her hands.

'You're in a land of magic,' she said, 'a land of sun and snow, and daylight and stars all at once. A land of friends and family, of love and laughter, of warmth and light, even inside a snowball or paper bag full of water thrown at you.' She stood up and danced across the floor, lightly and effortlessly. 'A land where everyone loves someone special, and rainfall

90

means running across the fields with your mouth open, laughing and screaming and falling over in the mud.' She opened a cupboard door and pulled out a rather strangely shaped globe. She held it up to him like a trophy. 'Art, whenever you're sad and wish you were somewhere you could be completely happy and do whatever you like and laugh about it, even if it's something really naughty, that place is here.' She walked over to the table and set the globe down.

The globe was a flat oval shape, fixed to a wooden stand with shiny brass screws and bolts. It showed mostly land painted in brown, with the occasional bit of sea in very light blue. The writing on it was almost the same as on the horn, but painted very carefully in black although sometimes a little smudged. Hité spun it on its spindle. Art realised that if this world was indeed oval shaped like the globe, that would explain why the moon may have been a different size when the paintings were created.

Hité stopped it spinning at a very large piece of land marked 'Amarly. Sal-Shet'.

'This is where we are,' she said. 'We've never been far away. We've been here right next to you for thousands of years. A lot of important work happens here that keeps the balance between what is right and what is fair, and makes you and your people very happy. This has been done for centuries and still nobody has found us.' She looked him in the eyes. 'Open your mind, Arthur. You know who we are. You just don't believe it yet.'

And just then the door opened and Scem strode in, rubbing his hands together.

'Come on, Art,' he said, 'we're all getting very impatient out here. It's ready!'

And Art was ushered outside just as he thought he was getting somewhere, and was engulfed in snow and icy wind.

Chapter Eight
The Unitor's Residence

Scem led Art down the steps of the Inn and along the little high street of the L-Shaped Village. They passed the food and hardware shop, and in the street was the 'horse' and cart that Art had seen from a distance the day before. They walked round it, and Art noticed that the sign for the L-Shaped Village Meeting Hall was lying broken up in the back of the cart. They passed a shop that he hadn't noticed before, probably because the whole shop front was so thick with snow and ice. It was Dorin and Son's Fortified Wine Collectors. The shop was in darkness and obviously closed. The window frames were painted a deep red colour, and the shop looked like it could be a cosy place to visit when it was open and doing business.

The next building along was the meeting hall where the villagers had gathered for Art's arrival the previous day, and they were out in force again today, all looking very excited about something. Standing as if on parade was a group of young men, all wearing a hat like Scem's with the same symbol on the side, and each carrying a 'Sta'an' in a sheath around their waists. Art could see the discipline on their faces, and he supposed that this was what was keeping them from looking as excited as the others. They stopped just short of the large door.

'Wait here, Art. We're just sorting out some last minute touches that we couldn't do until you were here,' Scem explained, before disappearing inside the building, leaving Art standing out in the cold with a hundred eyes on him.

The 'horse' and cart had caught up with them and stopped right next to Art. Art couldn't help but stare; it was huge. It looked like one big muscle, flexing and rippling under a coat of long brown shaggy hair. Its four legs shifted restlessly in the snow, its feet out of sight. Its head was nothing more than a big bump protruding from its bulbous body, with no apparent neck. It moved its body round slightly so that its big brown eyes could swivel in their sockets, and it looked at him expectantly. It made a low trumpet-like grunt as it strained in its harness to move towards him, and Art reached out a hand to pat its trunk-like arm. It grunted again, lower and more relaxed this time. Its huge hand grabbed a handful of snow and held it out to Art, who paused for a moment, and then accepted it.

'Thank you,' he said quietly.

The creature's eyes winked and it grunted again, trying to move even more in his harness. Art had a feeling this creature was a bit too intelligent to be used as a carthorse.

At that moment, Scem burst through the huge door and the crowd of villagers moved their attention to him. In his leader's voice, chest puffed out, he said, 'R-thor, Bottom Of Your Class At Most Things! We have kept your residence clean and tidy ever since we have had the Scriptures. And now they are ready to be used at last! Step this way, friend, and inspect your new quarters!'

Art could see that Scem's heart was not in it, the disappointment of the day before still weighing heavily on his mind, and he could also tell he was keeping up the pretence for Hité's sake. Art patted the animal and then moved towards the door. He peered inside. If it had indeed been a meeting hall the previous day, it bore no resemblance to one now. The room was extravagantly furnished and decorated, with a large fireplace similar to the one in The Horn Keeper Inn. There were numerous paintings on the walls showing himself emerging from the Sun and Snow Hut, with the sun and its red shadow moon accurately portrayed as they were in the sky right then. He looked back at the crowd of villagers and immediately spotted who must be Pedya, covered in paint, with wet easels hanging from his belt and looking gleefully happy with himself. Art thought the person standing next to him must be Jonnoe, covered in wood filings and still holding a worn-out and torn piece of sandpaper folded in two.

Art could smell Stroth-Brew and looked back into the room. Sure enough, on the table in the centre was a jug of something steaming hot, with several mugs surrounding it. He looked at Scem.

'This is really … I … I'm meant to live here?' he asked.

Scem turned to the villagers. 'I think he likes it!' he shouted.

A big cheer erupted on the streets, and as it died down Art heard someone shouting, although it was very faint. Scem heard it too, and they turned to see where it was coming from. Immediately, the crowd of villagers parted. Skiing towards them in the snow was a group of three more soldiers, wearing the characteristic warrior hats.

They shouted to Scem. 'Sir! Sir! Major problem on the other side of the lake!'

They skidded to a halt in front of Scem and drew their Sta'ans from their sheaths, holding them by the blunt little blades. He touched each of the carved wooden handles in turn, and the soldiers returned them to their sheaths.

Scem's manner changed such as Art had never seen. His voice was calm but strong, and somehow commanded great respect.

'Go on, Corporal, tell me what you know,' he said.

The soldier leant on his ski poles from exhaustion as he spoke, but was careful not to seem too casual in front of his commander.'

'We found one of Jo'Sys's soldiers on a routine patrol, and he told us of an attempt to take their town two days ago. It was completely surrounded by men bearing the Blue Triangle crest, and demands were given via an ambassador. They wanted immediate surrender of the village and access to all the intelligence regarding the Regional Armies, especially ours. They refused, of course. Jo'Sys sent out a unit of Fellsmen with orders to take them down, but when they engaged, they found the Blue Triangle troops were trained, sir. Highly trained in engagement. Half of Jo'Sys's men were

94

Felled before they regained control and had them fleeing. When they got back inside the perimeter they found that Jo'Sys had been taken. The remaining troops guarding him say three Blue Triangle troops rushed in at an impossible speed, grabbed him and escaped just as quickly. They were in and out before they could draw. They left some notes, one for each of the captains. The name is written in Blue Triangle ink, sir – it must be opened soon or it will fade and be taken as a non-response.'

Art was wondering what the soldier meant when he said that some of the men had been *felled* – but he didn't like the sound of it.

Scem accepted the envelope from the corporal, which was addressed to 'Scem of The L-Shaped Village' written in blue ink with a strange violet tinge.

'Thank you, Corporal. Take your post,' said Scem.

The three soldiers stepped out of their skis and slid over to the troop of men to take their positions amongst the ranks. They adopted the posture and composure of the other troops, and before long Art was unable to tell them apart.

Scem opened the letter and scanned the contents. He made no attempt to hide the contents of the letter from Art; Scem's name had been written on the front in clear English, but the letter inside was written in a strange language that Art could not decipher. Even stranger, some of the letters seemed to glow slightly as Art looked at them.

After a while, Scem muttered under his breath, '*Immediate surrender ... hostage returned* ...hmm, we'll see.' Then he screwed up the paper and threw it in the direction of the large 'horse'. Faster than was natural, the beast's long arm-like trunk snatched it out of the air and threw it over its head into its own cart.

Scem once again turned to his troops. 'Sergeant, I need your thoughts, and one of your best Fellspeople – we have a mission of the highest priority.'

95

Almost immediately, two men were standing in front of Scem with their Sta'ans drawn as the other soldiers had done. Scem touched the Sta'an of the slightly larger man, who re-sheathed.

'Thank you, Sergeant. There is no time to explain just now, but we must move quickly. This is your best junior Fellswoman I take it?'

Art looked again at the smaller of the two people who had stepped forward, only then realising her femininity. She was as well built as all the other troops in the squad, and it dawned on Art that the troop did not only comprise little men, but little women too, collectively so focused and disciplined that they all looked strikingly similar. Scem reached out to touch the handle of her Sta'an as she drew it, but Hité's hand found his and stopped him.

'Scem, my dear,' she said, 'you may not have need of your Fellswoman just now. Why don't you look a little closer to home?'

Scem thought for a second, then slowly turned and looked in Art's direction. Art was sure he saw Scem close his eyes as he realised what Hité meant. He tried to think up an excuse as to why he couldn't go, when Scem put his hand out for Art to shake.

'Ar-Thor will come too. This involves him as well,' he said.

Art was surprised by this outcome, but then he realised what Scem had done and shook his hand. Scem's quick-thinking had avoided embarrassment for himself, Hité, Art and the soldier who had stepped up. These were the kind of leadership skills Art wished he possessed, but knew he never would; they were instinctual skills that simply couldn't be taught. Scem touched the handle of the second soldier and she re-sheathed her weapon, flashing Art a cold look of pure anger as she did so. Although Hité wasn't looking in her direction, she noticed this, but refrained from reacting. Art reluctantly stepped in line with the two soldiers, and Scem lowered his voice to brief them.

'This may be a long voyage, nearly long enough to warrant the services of Captain Mercian's land ship. But we must hurry – we may not have time

96

to summon him. Sergeant, keep a wide field of thought on the way out in case you can sense him. If you can't, we'll proceed on foot. Private Calsow, keep your Sta'an drawn the whole way – you know the drill. Ar-Thor, observe and inform.'

His orders to Art were the simplest of those given, their purpose only to prevent Scem's failing beliefs in the Scriptures being aired in front of his men. He turned to his troop, still lined up like statues.

'Corporal Stack, I need provisions and equipment for up to three days in my hands in three minutes flat, go!'

One of the soldiers in the front row broke rank and darted around the back of the village at an impressive speed.

'Corporal Pannett,' Scem continued, 'you have the troop while I'm away. That means you have the village as well. You are to stay extra frosty. No need to double the guard, but you must report to Hité every hour, understood?'

Another of the female soldiers broke rank and rushed to the front of the squad.

'Not a problem, sir. Nothing will get past the perimeter,' she confirmed.

Hité walked over to Scem and touched his hand. He nodded and stepped aside. She walked up to Art, reached inside her tunic and withdrew a long, slender Sta'an made of the smoothest carved wood Art had ever seen. Hité offered the Sta'an to Art. Private Calsow seemed to dislike this gesture, and Art could feel her anger bubbling over.

'Captain Mercian left this for you on his first visit here.' said Hité. 'He said you would need it more than he,' she explained.

Art took the Sta'an from her with both hands, staring in awe at its sheer beauty.

'Th … thank you,' he managed to say. He stood staring at it for an uncomfortably long time.

Hité whispered to him, 'Your *sheath*, Art.'

He snapped out of his trance-like state and slid the Sta'an into the leather sheath at his side. It was a perfect fit. Calsow was visibly shaking now.

'Permission to speak, ma'am,' she said strongly.

Hité looked over at her.

'Of course, Shay-la,' she replied.

'That is *NOT* his Sta'an,' Shay-la spat. 'Using it will be an insult to the life-force. He hasn't followed the process – his Sta'an is meant to find *him*. With all due respect, ma'am, what are you *thinking*?'

Scem stepped in at once.

'Private, control yourself!' he said. 'Some things are above us all, and you will not question them.'

'But, sir...'

'That's enough, Private!' he interrupted.

Shay-la hushed at once and remained silent. Hité reached out and took her hand.

'Shay-la, I know what you must be thinking, as did I when Captain Mercian left it for Art. But he read the Scriptures and interpreted something I couldn't. And whatever got his attention made him leave his Sta'an under my protection until this day. Shay-la, you must *trust* me. Can you do that?'

Shay-la looked a little more at ease, but was still angry.

'I can,' she said, 'but I don't have to like it. Jonnoe will not be happy about this.'

'I know,' replied Hité, 'but he trusts me as you do.'

Shay-la's eyes widened.

'He *knows*?' she said, incredulous.

'Not yet, but he will. He doesn't miss a thing.' Hité's expression went vacant for a second. 'Oh, actually he's just seen it,' she said.

Shay-la looked back at the villagers, searching for Jonnoe. She spotted him almost immediately – he was wearing a look of shock and bewilderment.

Hité patted Shay-la's hand. 'He'll come round,' she said.

Corporal Stack returned to the front of the troop as quickly as he had left, and four brilliant white backpacks lay at their feet.

'All's in order, sir,' he said, and darted back amongst the ranks.

Scem faced his small contingent. 'Say your goodbyes, Private. Sergeant, sprint ahead to the hut and wait for us there.'

The sergeant slung his backpack around onto his back and darted off in the direction Art had come from the previous day. Shay-la gave Art a caustic look, her eyes darting to the Sta'an at his side; then she too darted off, but in the direction of the villagers.

Scem openly took Hité in his arms and held her tightly.

'I'll be back before you know it,' he said.

Art felt slightly embarrassed at this open display of affection and turned his gaze towards the villagers. He could see Shay-la finding Jonnoe and holding him as Scem held Hité. *They must be a couple too*, he thought. He wondered why the sergeant hadn't said goodbye to anyone. He looked back at the tracks in the snow he had made and was surprised by how far he had already gone, heading straight for the Sun and Snow Hut. And then, only a few seconds later, Shay-la was back and Scem was offering Art one of the backpacks.

'We must go,' said Scem, and together they strode off briskly, following the sergeant's tracks. When they were a hundred yards or so away, Art heard some orders being barked, presumably by Corporal Pannett, and he could just make out three soldiers leaving the village on skis in three different directions. Then the village was out of sight, lost in a thin dusting of snow falling from the sky, and Art was alone with two people who wished he had never arrived.

Chapter Nine

Oro and Hiro

Slowly, the Sun and Snow Hut came into view. It was snowing heavily, and Art could see no sign of the sunny weather that had welcomed him when he had approached it from the other side the previous day. Suddenly, he realised he was walking on soft green grass with the sun beating down on his head. He stopped and turned round, trying to work out what had happened. He couldn't believe his eyes. The snow had simply stopped; there was none on the ground and, more surprisingly, none falling from the sky. He could see some on the ground where he had come from, and he could see it falling from the sky there too, but there seemed to be a barrier separating the two weather systems. He could hardly believe his eyes.

'Sir,' the sergeant's voice boomed as he emerged from the Hut, 'everything is clear. But still no sign of Captain Mercian or the Picasso. We can move out when you're ready.' He held the door open for them.

Art was dressed as he was when he had arrived, and the Fragment was still radiating heat through his whole being. He was so used to it he had forgotten it was still keeping him warm. The others, however, were all wearing thick garments to keep them warm, and when they entered the Hut they began removing these and shaking off the snow. A fire crackled in the grate. They all hung up their garments and then gathered around the table. The sergeant pulled a kettle of boiling water from over the fire and made four tankards of Stroth-Brew.

'Here,' said Scem, handing Art a little wooden box he had fished pulled out of his backpack. 'Hité gave me this for you.'

Inside was a little glass jar of thin honey and a small stopper-bottle of milk. Art smiled, and for the first time since they had left the village he noticed a flicker of a smile from Scem too. He put a little of each into his tankard, and stirred the liquid with the little silver oar Hité had also packed for him. Before long, the smell of Art's particular version of Stroth-Brew was affecting the others - all but Shay-la, who refused to show any reaction. Scem and the sergeant were looking at his little Stroth-Brew condiments kit and soon, the sergeant could restrain himself no longer.

'Art, erm, do you mind?' he asked, nodding towards the little box.

'Please do,' said Art, and before long they both had pale sweet-smelling drinks, the aroma of which filled the room.

Shay-la was looking uncomfortable, and Art felt a little sorry for her. He reached over to her tankard with the honey pot and tried to gauge her reaction. Nothing. So he poured a little in, then a little milk, and handed her the oar. She took it without saying anything and stirred the mix. She dropped the oar and took a sip. She tried hard not to show any emotion, but Art was sure she was surprised by how much better it tasted. They all sat in silence for a short while until they had all drained their tankards, despite the supposed importance of their mission.

At last, Scem turned to business. He pulled a map from inside his tunic and spread it out on the tabletop.

'So – we are *here*,' he said, pointing to the edge of a white circle on the map. There was a little dot labelled *S & S*. 'And we need to get to ... *here*.' He pointed to the other end of the map, where there were several caves labelled *Shalmani Caves*. 'If need be, we can stop off in Trade Town along the way.'

Art noticed Trade Town was just above the caves on the map.

'When we get there,' Scem continued, 'we're to meet with a contingent of Blue Triangle troops, who should be in the third cave. Calsow, I need your Sta'an at the ready as soon as we leave – I'm not taking any chances.'

The sergeant opened his mouth to speak, but Scem cut him off.

'I know what you're thinking, Sergeant, and it had crossed my mind too. It could all be a distraction to get me out of the village.'

101

'What if it is, sir?' the sergeant asked.

'Then I'm not worried. Pannett is perfectly capable of defending the perimeter. You should know, Sergeant – you trained her.'

'I understand that, sir, but what if YerDichh is slowing time like Jo'Sys described?' he replied.

'That can't happen,' Shay-la cut in.

'That's right, Private,' Scem said.

'Why's that?' asked the sergeant.

'The L-Shaped Village houses the only *naturally* occurring Collection Point known to exist. Time cannot, or will not, be altered around it. That's why Pud and Jimma's entry route to the village is so far out. I don't think YerDichh has realised that yet.'

Art gasped. He knew exactly what Scem was talking about – the woods where he had encountered the vicious cat-type animals.

'Is that … is that where...' he began.

Scem almost beamed at him. But only almost.
'That's right, Art. And come to think of it, that may be the reason YerDichh is so interested in the L-Shaped Village.'

'Who is *YerDichh*, anyway?' asked Art.

Shay-la sighed deeply, annoyed at Art's ignorance.

'Sir, is it really necessary to have *him* with us? He's going in blind, and he doesn't even know how to use ... *his* ... weapon. If you ask me, he's endangering the mission,' she droned.

'Hold your tongue, Private. Remember what I said to you before. Sergeant, if you please.'

The sergeant turned his chair slightly towards Art and leant on the table, while Scem went over to the fire to refill his tankard.

'No one really knows exactly *who* YerDichh is or where he came from, but rumour has it he was born right here in Amarly,' the sergeant explained. "He never found his Ferling and his skill never revealed itself. He has no Sta'an, no amulet of any sort, and no traceable roots.'

102

Art didn't understand the word *Ferling* or the relevance of a skill, but he thought better than to ask just now.

'There's never been anyone with no obvious skill and no Ferling before,' Scem said.

'But why is he a problem?' asked Art.

Shay-la snorted.

'Again, no one really knows,' said the sergeant. 'He just can't leave anything alone. He interferes with anything he can, and when he is politely asked to mind his own business, he turns nasty.'

'Exactly right, Sergeant.' said Scem. 'But five years ago he disappeared without warning, and returned just last year under the guise of the Commander of the Blue Triangle Army.'

'The Blue Triangle Army?' said Art.

'That's right,' continued Scem. 'It's thought that he overtook a small settlement on the outskirts of Amarly and persuaded them to form the Battalion under his command. I don't know what he said to them, but ever since, they've been trying to unravel the secrets of Pud and Jimma's research and its resulting technology. There have been several attempts to infiltrate the Headquarters, but of course it's impossible. Pud and Jimma are too clever.'

Shay-la suddenly stood up.

'That's why they're going for the CP in the L-Shaped Village!' she cried.

'Even though ours is *naturally* occurring, Private, yes. They think they'll have more of a chance with us, even though Pud and Jimma's comes with an instruction manual,' Scem explained.

Art handed Scem his condiment kit, and he nodded his thanks.

'Well, it's obvious to me,' said Art. 'It *must* be a trap. Doesn't that worry you?'

Scem looked a little surprised by Art's unexpected contribution.

'Well of course it does. Who knows what he wants with it. And imagine what he *could* do with it.'

103

Shay-la looked worried.

'What could he do with it?' Art asked.

Shay-la confronted him.

'It's a naturally occurring *Positional Time-Portal*, you idiot! He could go AnyTime-Where and change anything he likes! It's bad enough that Pud and Jimma created their own Portal, but at least that can be destroyed!'

Scem seemed to understand her outburst this time and placed a hand on her shoulder. She became a little calmer and sat back down.

'Needless to say, Art, the consequences are unthinkable. But I have confidence in Corporal Pannett. We're here to find out *why* he wants it, and the whole *point* is to spring the trap to do it. The sergeant here is a twin, which means they won't suspect he has *two* skills – a Fellsman is skill enough. He'll be able to read them and they won't suspect a thing.'

'So what are we waiting for?' said Art.

Shay-la looked almost impressed by his eagerness, and Scem grinned.

'Now, now, we can't go in unprepared. You haven't even tried Captain Mercian's Sta'an yet. Private Calsow, you're up.'

Private Calsow stood up, looking outraged.

'Don't even *try* it,' scolded Scem.

She closed her eyes, trying to control her anger, and swept out of the Hut.

*

Scem and the sergeant sat outside the Hut, watching Shay-la's lesson. They both had full tankards in their hands and were wearing amused expressions. Art and Shay-la were stood ten yards away from them, facing one another. Art looked uncomfortable; Shay-la looked angry at best.

'Maybe a small demonstration will best show you what a Sta'an can do,' she said, and with that she drew her Sta'an from her sheath and held it out in front of her at a forty-five degree angle, her hand rock-steady.

104

Art saw her expression become calm and she exhaled sharply. Art felt a huge bass rumble beneath his feet, and as he looked down to see what was happening, both his feet were pulled out forwards from underneath him by an unseen force, that kind of felt like a strong river; and he fell to the floor in confusion. Shay-la stood with one leg behind the other, with her Sta'an held as if she was ready to strike again. She slowly sheathed it, a look of anger on her face.

'Did you catch all that, or do I need to show you again?' she sneered.

'I think I've got it, thanks,' Art replied, as he tried to get up.

'Ah - ah,' shouted Scem from his ring-side seat, wagging his finger. 'It's very bad etiquette to right oneself once you've been felled...' Art's legs were pulled from under him again, slightly more forcefully this time. He hadn't even noticed Shay-la had drawn her Sta'an again.

'How *dare* you,' she spat. Scem and the Sergeant sniggered.

'You *never* get up - it's obscenely rude,' she carried on.

'But this is a sort of fight, isn't it? Why can't I get back up?' he Art replied.

'No one has *ever* got up,' she said incredulously.

Art leant on his elbows. 'And everyone follows this rule?' he said.

'Well of course they do. Why would they not?'

'Oh, I don't know – maybe to *win*?' he retorted.

Shay-la laughed at this.

'If you fall, you've lost already, *boy*.' She exaggerated a bow in his direction. 'Now stand up.'

Art rose slowly to his feet. Shay-la re-sheathed her Sta'an and walked over to him.

'Now let's see if we can't teach you something,' she sneered. 'Take out your Sta'an and hold it firmly by the handle.'

Art did as he was told, holding it at an angle as she had.

'You don't have to hold it out like that if you don't want to, just do whatever feels most comfortable.'

Art moved it around a bit, but felt no discernible difference.

'Now, close your eyes. Feel the shimmer of the wood, its power.'

Art concentrated, but felt nothing. He thought he heard the tiniest snippet of voices coming from somewhere, but they were gone in a second.

'Do you feel it?' Shay-la asked.

Art couldn't feel it. He couldn't feel anything.

'Imagine there is a thread just in front of you, with a loop. It's a gold thread, and you know it's strong, unbreakable. Think hard.' She breathed deeply and Art did the same, though he didn't understand why.

'Convince yourself the thread is tied around your opponent's ankles, or knees. Feel the loop with the end of your Sta'an. Picture it, *will* the loop into being.' She paused. 'Is it there?' she asked.

'Erm, I … I think so,' he lied.

'Good. Imagine it's been part of your Sta'an the whole time. Keep it still. Ever so still. You must concentrate. Breathe.' She breathed deeply again. Art followed her lead. 'Build the power, a warm golden glow of energy, and send it down the thread. Feel the energy. Then when you're sure it's secure, pull the weapon back hard and fast, believing all the way. Belief is the strongest weapon in your arsenal.'

Art still felt like he was just holding a random piece of wood in his hand, listening to a fairytale. He felt stupid.

'You're not concentrating,' Shay-la said impatiently. 'If you don't concentrate, you'll lose. You don't have time for games.'

She drew her Sta'an with impossible speed and Art felt the rumble again. She whipped it back with precision and grace, and Art prepared for the inevitable, keeping his eyes closed in humiliation, waiting for the river to sweep his feet away. He braced himself this time, hoping to somehow cushion the fall, but all he felt was the slight chill from the weather on the other side of the Hut and the sun on his face. He opened his eyes. Shay-la, Scem and the sergeant were staring at him open-mouthed. He was still standing.

Scem scrambled up from the floor, letting his tankard fall to the ground. He walked over to them, the sergeant hot on his tail.

'Wh ... what did you do?' Scem asked Art, but Art didn't have the answer.

Shay-la's expression turned from surprise to anger and she repositioned her Sta'an. Art felt the rumble under his feet and saw Shay-la grit her teeth and whip back her Sta'an behind her head with frightening speed as she exhaled sharply. Again, nothing happened. Art saw a small smile break out on Scem's face.

'I don't believe it,' he said.

His whole demeanour seemed to change, almost back to how it had been when they first met. Shay-la looked utterly bewildered. The sergeant unsheathed his Sta'an and Shay-la stepped out of the way. He held his Sta'an with both hands in the middle of his chest, half-closed his eyes, muttered a few unfamiliar syllables and then Art felt the same rumbling beneath his feet. The sergeant turned on the spot, finishing with his Sta'an still in the middle of his chest but facing the other way. His style was totally different to Shay-la's, but again, nothing happened.

Scem laughed, a look of glee on his face.

'Art, that was fantastic!' he said.

Art still had no idea what he had done. All he knew was that Shay-la had felled him once, but her further *two* attempts had failed, and so had the sergeant's. Her and the sergeant sheathed their weapons, shocked.

'We have protection!' shouted Scem. 'This is unheard of! This is unprecedented! Oh-my-gosh-oh-my-gosh! We must investigate this!' He ran over and stood a few feet behind Art, who still had his own Sta'an drawn.

'Private, take us down. That's an order!'

Commander or not, Shay-la was not one to disobey an order like this, and she drew her Sta'an. Moments later, the river was tugging at Art's feet, but with no effect. However, behind him, Scem's feet were pulled into the air and he crashed to the floor.

107

'It's still good, it's still good!' he said, though he made no attempt to right himself.

Shay-la sheathed her Sta'an and bowed her head. This seemed to be the signal Scem was waiting for, and he sprang to his feet.

'We still have one of our party who can't be felled! This is amazing news! How do you do it, Art?'

Art stared at his Sta'an, utterly perplexed.

'Never mind, never mind! One more little test, I think. Sergeant, Private, stand by me,' Scem instructed, and skipped across to where Shay-la had been standing moments earlier. He was joined by his two soldiers. 'One co-ordinated effort, I think! Let's see how much he can stand!'

All three drew their weapons, poised and ready to strike in their own styles. Scem's was the only one Art hadn't seen yet, and he stood with his arms apart like he was welcoming a friend, his Sta'an clasped in his left hand pointing to the sky. They concentrated in their own ways, Scem taking a deep breath and slowly closing his eyes.

'On streetia,' he said. 'Unurtia, doustia, *streetia!*'

They each made their strike simultaneously. Scem simply clapped his hands together, and Art noticed a wave of sound and a slight wind hit his face as he did so. He hadn't felt this when Shay-la and the sergeant had tried to Fell him, and was sure being Felled by Scem would be an unpleasant experience. He even felt slightly unsteady on his feet, but still he wasn't Felled.

A smile spread across Scem's face, wide and contagious. He looked like the little man Art had spotted through the snow-covered window again. He sheathed his Sta'an and strolled up to Art.

'My friend, I am sorry I doubted you. So very sorry.' He took Art's hand and shook it violently; he wasn't afraid of showing his remorse at his doubt the previous day in front of the others. 'Captain Mercian's weapon is a fine one indeed! Sergeant, we move in two minutes – we've done all the preparation we need!'

Art was still unsure what had just happened.

'I really don't see what I've done,' he said. 'I haven't even learnt to use the Sta'an yet.'

Scem put his hand on Art's shoulder.

'I'm starting to see what Hité meant now – you *are* great, Art, but for some higher reason you don't know it yet. What we've just witnessed has *never* been done before. The only way to defend against Felling is to be faster than your opponent. There *is* no way to stop it other than to get in there first. But you *did*, Art. It's simply unheard of. Shay-la has almost unparalleled skill as a warrior on her own, but even against all *three* of us you remained upright. This is very exciting.'

Art was more confused than ever. He looked at his weapon; it still felt like a useless piece of wood he'd picked up from a woodland floor.

'But I still can't use this,' he said.

'Oh, but you can! And what *you* can do is far more useful. When we meet YerDichh's contingent of men, I can guarantee that one of us will be left standing if it comes to a confrontation. We have the upper hand! Come on – let's grab the packs and we'll head off.'

Art still had one burning question. When he had heard the troops explaining to Scem about the attack on Trade Town back in the L-Shaped Village, they had explained how many men had been Felled, and he didn't like the sound of it. He had thought the worst, but now it just sounded like a big game of Sleeping Tigers.

'So ... Felling just means being thrown to the floor? There's nothing more to it than that?' Art said.

Scem looked serious again. 'We are a very honourable people, Art. Battles are fought and won, and even lost, on the basis of an unwavering conscience on both sides. So yes, there is absolutely nothing more to it than that. If it turns nasty and we're all Felled, then we absolutely *will* yield.' He patted him on the back. 'But it won't come to that – not after this! Come, friend, we have a meeting to attend.'

109

Shay-la appeared from the Hut carrying both her and Art's pack. The sergeant was carrying Scem's and his own.

'We'll split into two, travelling fifty sents apart,' Scem said. 'Myself and the sergeant will take point. Let's go.' Scem donned his pack and headed off directly away from the direction of the L-Shaped Village, the sergeant keeping up with strong steady steps.

Shay-la cleared her throat next to Art.

'Erm, I packed your tankard. And your gourd of milk and honey.' She handed Art his pack sheepishly. She seemed to have warmed to him slightly, but was still very wary.

'Thanks,' he said, and swung it around onto his back.

Shay-la gauged Scem's distance and nodded in his direction.

'We should go,' she said. 'Stay next to me, and keep up.' She took off at a surprisingly brisk pace for her size, but Art's larger gait made it easy for him to stay with her.

They were heading along a path that ran directly next to the woods Art had initially found himself in, and he could even see the little path leading back into the trees. He could make out some large mountains in the distance; two stood out as being much larger and topped with snow and fog. Shay-la saw him looking at them, clearly in awe.

'We're headed directly in between those. They're called Oro and Hiro. Hiro's on the right.' She reached into her tunic pocket and pulled out two light brown sticks of dried bread. 'Here,' she said, handing one over.

Art took it with a smile, and he was sure he saw the slightest glimmer of a smile in return.

After a while they reached the top of a grassy hill. They hadn't exchanged a word, but Art felt comfortable, and he could tell that the silence wasn't bothering Shay-la either. His mind wandered back to something that had puzzled him just before leaving the village, and he broke the silence.

'Shay-la, why didn't the sergeant have anyone to say goodbye to back there?'

110

She didn't say anything for a moment, and Art thought that perhaps he shouldn't have interrupted the comfort of their silent and purposeful walk. But then he noticed a smile blossom on her face, with her eyes as much as her mouth.

'Sergeant has no Ferling yet. It's okay – you don't miss the comfort it brings unless you're coupled.'

Art thought for a moment.

'So Jonnoe is your Ferling?' he asked.

She looked at him, almost impressed. 'That's right, but Sergeant isn't coupled. At least not yet.'

'I haven't caught his name,' Art said. 'Aren't you allowed to call him by his name?'

'Not when I'm on duty, no. But Scem does all the time. His last name actually *is* Sergeant.' She laughed when Art looked confused.

'So he's...'

'Sergeant *Sergeant*, yes!'

Now Art was laughing. 'Does he have a first name?' he asked.

Shay-la glared at him as if he had said something rude.

'What is it?' he said.

She sniggered. 'Lance.'

Art nearly spat out some of his breadstick.

'You're kidding me!' he laughed.

'Believe me, it was even funnier when he was a corporal!'

They were beginning to sound like old friends, and it was a surprising but welcome change for Art.

'He's a good man, though,' she continued, 'and he was born to be a sergeant. Literally, I think. He's nothing like Hité.'

'What do you mean?' said Art.

She have him a sideways glance. 'You're a bit slow, aren't you? He's a twin. He's a Fellsman and a Mind-Charm. Do the maths.'

Art raised his eyebrows. 'He's *Hité's* twin?'

111

'There it is,' she said, grinning.

Art suddenly realised why he had recognised some of the looks Sergeant gave him. He didn't have Hité's lisp, but he turned his head to the side whenever he was thinking about something, just like she did. It came as a bit of a shock, and Art felt silly that he hadn't seen it before. It certainly explained why he felt so comfortable in Sergeant's company; he never spoke to Art with any contempt or malice, and showed him the same silent respect Hité always had. They looked and acted so similar; how had he *not* noticed?

'That makes sense,' he said finally. 'Is that why Sergeant and Scem seem to get on so well?'

Shay-la nearly looked annoyed. 'That has *nothing* to do with it,' she said firmly. 'And it has nothing to do with his rank either, before you ask.' She was clearly offended.

'I wasn't going to say that,' he said quickly. 'I'm sorry.'

'He's an excellent sergeant, the best there's been. That's why Scem chose him, nothing else.'

Art thought for a moment. 'So there are other armies then?' he said.

'In a way, yes. There's a troop of soldiers for each group of settlements. Ours covers the L-Shaped Village, the River Settlement and the Valley. Jo'Sys's troop covers Trade Town and the Plains.' She seemed a bit happier talking about this. 'When Sergeant's Sta'an found him, he was called away to Trade Town as a trainee soldier. It broke Hité's heart, but it wasn't long before his reputation leaked and Scem sent for him.'

'And he can do that?' asked Art.

'Of course he can. The leader of the troop that controls the Centre for Collection is the leader of all troops by default. Scem is the Commander of the Unified Armies of Amarly. When he sent for Sergeant, Jo'Sys had no choice but to release him. He wasn't happy, I can tell you.'

'What's a Centre for Collection?' he asked.

Shay-la's playful smile returned.

'I can't tell you that,' she said.

112

'You've been lectured by Hité as well then?'

'We all have. I was sceptical at first.' She looked slightly embarrassed. 'I'm sorry by the way, about how I've been treating you. It's just ... Captain Mercian's Sta'an is ... special to me.'

'Oh, that's okay. To be honest I don't really know what all the fuss is about,' Art replied.

Shay-la looked shocked. 'Well you should! What you did back there, it was ... well it was ... just impossible.'

Art scoffed. 'I don't even know what I did.' He drew his Sta'an and inspected it. 'I have no idea what any of this is.' Unsheathing his Sta'an had a visible effect on Shay-la.

'A Sta'an is the most valuable possession imaginable. It only happens once in a lifetime, and it stays with you forever. Your own Sta'an has it's own character, kind of like an extension of your own. It seems to *know* you, it gets inside you, it gives you the confidence to do things *your* way. Your own Sta'an is like no other, and the feelings you develop for it because of that are with you forever. You become inseparable. No two have *ever* been the same. Well, not until...' She drew her Sta'an and held it beside Art's.

It took him a while to see what he was looking at. They were identical, not just in the way they were carved but in every way, including the most impossible way. The grain of the wood was perfectly matched, every line and curve identical, the colours indistinguishable. They could be the same Sta'an, but Art knew that the grain of any wood was as individual as a fingerprint, and even more individual than DNA. It simply wasn't possible.

'They called us both together. He arrived all those years ago, out of nowhere as you did. I'll never forget wondering why he could hear my calling, until I realised. They were calling us both, at the same time. The same dying oak, two parts of the same last living branch, calling us as one, but with two voices. No one could believe it.' She started to well up.

'That's why you were so annoyed at me having this Sta'an?' Art said.

113

Shay-la nodded. 'I'm sorry,' she said. 'It's part of a very special pair. That's never happened before either. But when I saw what you could do with it, I knew why he'd left it. I have no idea why, but he must have known it would know you. I'm sorry,' she said again. 'I didn't even know he'd left it with Hité until she gave it to you. It was a bit of a shock.'

'Well it seems obvious to me who it belongs with,' he said.

Shay-la perked up. 'What do you mean?'

'When this is over, *you* must guard it for Captain Mercian until he reclaims it.'

Shay-la gasped. In an instant she had re-sheathed her Sta'an and was embracing Art with surprising strength.

'Thank you,' she said quietly into his shoulder.

And that's when he saw it. In the distance, Scem and Sergeant were both Felled in the most spectacular manner and lay quite still on the floor. Shay-la pulled away from Art and saw the shock in his eyes.

Chapter Ten

Engagement

Shay-la didn't even look to see what had happened; her training took over and she threw herself and Art to the side of the path using the grip she already had on him. Together they scrambled behind a thick gorse bush, and Shay-la drew her Sta'an with frightening speed.

'Draw!' she whispered loudly, and Art pulled out his Sta'an rather more clumsily. She pushed aside some of the branches and narrowed her eyes. 'Both down. They're okay, but Felled. No sign of the attackers – they must be good to do it from so far out.'

'We should go and help…' Art began.

'No!' Shay-la grabbed him as he began to move. 'They might be waiting to see if they're alone. They'd Fell us as soon as we showed. Best plan for now is to wait.'

'We can't just leave them there! We've got to help!'

'Stay where you are!' Shay-la growled. 'Trust me.'

Art settled back on his haunches and waited. He noticed he was breathing heavily, but Shay-la was calm and controlled, her concentration focused on the problem in hand.

After a minute or two there was movement from the side of the path next to Scem and Sergeant. Two figures emerged from the bushes and walked up to the Felled pair.

'It was a trap!' Shay-la whispered. 'And they were right next to them, hardly anything special at all – they Felled them from a few feet away.'

The taller of the figures scanned the horizon in all directions, but he clearly didn't see Art and Shay-la.

Shay-la turned to Art. 'This is going to be easy. Best plan – I'll crawl around the outside and take them out from behind. But it's going to need a diversion. I want you to walk out there and distract them.'

'Are you crazy?' Art screamed in a whisper. 'I'm not going out there!'

'You have to. Do you want to help them or not?'

Art looked through the bushes to where Scem and Sergeant lay, and closed his eyes.

'Okay, okay.'

'Good. Nice and bold, now. You'll be fine – you can't be Felled, remember? And you must keep their attention, okay? Art!'

'Yeah, okay! Just … give me a minute.' *What am I doing?* Art thought. He took some deep breaths, steadied himself, held out his Sta'an and emerged from the bush.

He was spotted immediately, and both figures jumped into battle position, each with their own personal stance. He started walking towards them and noticed a slight rustle of the bushes to his right; Shay-la had already made her move – she was fast. She'd be behind them in no time at all. As he got closer, he saw Scem and Sergeant lying on the floor, fully conscious and unhurt, but motionless.

When Art was no more than ten feet away, he felt the familiar feeling of a river tugging at his feet. It tickled. The taller of the two made his strike, drawing his Sta'an back behind himself and finishing with his arms spread wide. Art saw a look of horror spread across the faces of the two men, while a look of smugness appeared on Scem's and Sergeant's.

Both attackers were wearing long grey cloaks adorned with a large blue triangle on the front and back, with blue sheaths around their waists. The second man made his strike, still wearing his look of horror. Again, Art stayed upright. Scem stifled a laugh.

'I … I don't understand. How…' the taller one stammered.

And just then, the smaller of the two seemed to jump into the air feet first and came crashing down on his back. Shay-la was standing behind them and

116

she readied her Sta'an for a second strike. She'd managed to Fell him *forwards* from behind. Art hadn't even seen her appear.

'Hold your position!' she shouted, short and sharp.

The taller man froze, feeling the river tugging at his feet. Shay-la edged around him and rejoined Art, keeping her Sta'an fixed and steady on her opponent.

'You're outnumbered. Sheath your weapon.'

He did as he was told, then raised his hands. As soon as his Sta'an was fully sheathed, Scem and Sergeant sprang to their feet; Art quietly noted this rule of engagement.

'I am Dabellar of the Blue Triangle Army. I want to talk, nothing more.'

Shay-la didn't lower her Sta'an.

'Is that why you Felled my companions? That was *talking*, was it?' she said angrily.

Dabellar grinned. Shay-la pulled slightly on her Sta'an and his grin vanished.

'Talk out of turn once more and you'll be on your back,' Shay-la said with poison in her voice.

Art immediately disliked Dabellar and was glad Shay-la was there to keep him in check, even if she was being a little harsh in his opinion.

'State your purpose here,' said Scem, walking around the back of Shay-la so she could keep her hold on Dabellar.

'I take it Jo'Sys delivered the letter. Such an easy victory, such a pathetic little town.'

Shay-la sneered at him, but Scem placed a calming hand on her shoulder.

'I will ask you once more, state your purpose.'

Dabellar eyed Scem with disgust and sighed.

'YerDichh has a offer for you. An opportunity to surrender the secrets of the Portal peacefully, with full access.'

117

'Not happening,' said Scem with finality. 'Did you really think it would be that easy? And did you really think I would leave the L-Shaped Village unprotected?'

'I do as I am told. I have delivered the request; what is your answer, Commander?'

'You've had it. What say you to that?' said Scem, with a slight smile.

'I say you were foolish to even come here.'

Sergeant's eyes widened and he gasped. Art noticed the glimmer of a small droplet as it fell from Dabellar's free hand and splashed to the floor. Art was surrounded by a loud roar of wind and Dabellar rushed forward in an almost invisible blur. Suddenly, Scem, Sergeant, Shay-la and Art were weaponless, and facing two upright and armed Blue Triangle soldiers once more. The low wind stopped and the two troops came back into focus. Dabellar was grinning again, but with a raw kind of nastiness in his eyes that made Art sick to the stomach.

'Oh dear, I didn't think complacency was one of your weak points, Commander,' Dabellar said, waving a little stopper-bottle of clear liquid under their noses. He threw all four captured Sta'ans behind him, relishing in the anger on Shay-la's face.

Art realised at once what had happened. Somehow YerDichh knew he wouldn't be able to slow time near the village, and that Scem would be confident about leaving the village in the hands of his troops. He just needed to get Scem far enough away from the Portal to slow time and force him to yield. It seemed so simple now that it had happened; why had they not thought of it before?

'This is an outrage!' sneered Scem. 'You are ignoring the rules of engagement! A battle must be won fairly! What are you *doing*?'

Dabellar's grin grew wider. 'Now, now, Commander, I don't want to Fell you.'

Art felt a slow pulse from his wrist. He looked down and saw the Fragment still secure, pulling on his arm and urging him forward. He saw a

118

strange glow emanating from it, but no warmth this time. Something else. Something felt, sensed. It made him feel confident, brave, focused; and slightly annoyed. Annoyed with the triviality of these rules of engagement everyone seemed to be blindly following. How the simple act of who Felled who first was about to determine who gained control of a very dangerous time portal, if he even *believed* in its existence yet. It seemed so silly that Scem, Sergeant and Shay-la were about to yield, even more so now that Dabellar had broken these silly rules. Someone had to see sense in all of this and stop something stupid happening for fear of breaking a few codes of conduct. He looked up at Dabellar, his terrible grin sickening him, his very existence a distraction. A distraction to be removed, quickly and easily. The human way.

'I'll tell you what he's doing,' Art said. 'He's using your rules against you. He's breaking them. And so am I.'

Then Art did something that he would regret for the rest of his days. He walked forward and hit Dabellar square in the face. There was a sickening crunch of bone on bone and Dabellar fell to the floor, his eyes wide and confused.

*

'NO!' Scem screamed, and dragged Art back fiercely.

Everyone else was frozen in position, with looks of pure terror carved into their faces. Dabellar was crawling backwards away from Art, his nose bleeding badly.

'WHAT DID … HOW … WHAT DID YOU DO?' Scem screamed again, clearly not understanding what he had seen.

'I … er … fixed the situation,' Art said, starting to feel a bit unsure of himself after everyone's over-reaction. 'Come on, someone had to do something sensible.'

119

'SENSIBLE? I'VE NEVER SEEN … WHATEVER IT IS YOU DID!'

Dabellar was scrambling to his feet, helped by the as yet unknown smaller man. They grabbed their Sta'ans, which had flown out of their hands in the confusion, and backed away, keeping Art in their sight as they went. They were petrified, shaking and white as a sheet. They eventually disappeared from sight around the side of a hill and Art was left with the most deafening silence he had ever experienced.

Scem grabbed Art's shoulders and fronted up to him.

'What was that?' he asked hurriedly.

Art was starting to feel he had made a mistake as he tried to justify what he had just done.

'Somebody had to do something. This is silly, I only hit him.'

'Hit? Is that what you call it? Hitting? That's something you do to a nail with a hammer, or a rock with a chisel, never to a … a person, let alone by another person! I don't understand – what in Amarly possessed you to try that?'

There was wild confusion in Scem's eyes, and Art was beginning to think that these people had actually *never* seen anything like it before. He was incredulous. True, he had never started a fight before, but he had run away from a few. The only time he had ever stood his ground was when he saw three boys from Walt's year group holding Walt up against the wall around the back of the school trying to steal the computer game he had got for his birthday. Art wasn't the biggest in his year group and these boys were easily as tall as him, and much more thickset. He had ended up with a black eye for that, and it had scared him out of his wits. Today, though, he had felt a combination of incredible confidence and immense irritation. But the confidence was ebbing away by the second due to Scem's reaction.

Scem let him go and sat down on the floor with a bump, as though he had misjudged the distance. Shay-la wandered over to the fallen Sta'ans and collected them up, her movements slow and clumsy. She walked back to

Sergeant and handed him the wrong Sta'an. He took it without looking and sheathed it.

'What ... what did he do?' she managed to ask him.

'I ... well he ... moved his closed hand forward, with someone in the way. Yes, I ... I think that's what he did.'

Art was beginning to understand the absolute confusion all of them were feeling at what had happened, and even though he couldn't believe it, a sharp pang of guilt started to build up inside him.

'Scem,' he said, putting a hand on his shoulder, 'I was only trying to stop YerDichh from getting his hands on the Portal. I'm sorry...'

Scem was staring wildly into the distance, his breathing shallow and rapid. Shay-la was turning pale, her hands shaking. Sergeant seemed to be dealing with the situation slightly better, but even he wasn't himself.

'Lance, please...' Art pleaded, 'we have to do something.'

Sergeant started slightly, coming out of his stupor enough to realise Art was talking to him.

'Yes, of course ... we, err ... we must go.' He walked over to Scem and helped him up, then put an arm around Shay-la and managed to lead them both away, all three looking shaken and pale.

Art followed, still confused by the way they were taking it. The sight of Sergeant helping Scem and Shay-la to walk was a sorry one, especially as Scem was usually so alert and purposeful. Art was beginning to think he had seriously misjudged the way of things here, and the more he thought about it, the more he realised he had made the kind of mistake that would haunt him forever.

On the way back to the Hut, Sergeant seemed to recover, but Scem and Shay-la were still as silent and pale as before. Sergeant led them inside, sat them both at the table and set about making a pan of Stroth-Brew. Art followed them in and sat at the very edge of the table, wary of causing a reaction. Scem looked up and caught his eye, but Art could make out no discernible emotion. Shay-la laid her head on folded arms and closed her eyes. Soon the Hut was full of the smell of fresh Stroth-Brew, with the last of the milk and honey from Art's condiment kit. Sergeant gently pulled Shay-la upright and placed her fingers around the handle of her tankard. She looked at it, then took a sip. Scem did the same, but both were still looking vacant and seemingly unable to talk. Sergeant handed Art his tankard, then sat down himself. He warmed his hands on the vessel but did not drink.

'I think I know what happened,' Sergeant said at last.

Art almost jumped at the break in silence.

'I … I'm sorry, I really am … if I'd known…'

'It's okay,' Sergeant cut in, 'nobody was prepared. Hité tried to tell me how different things can be in your world, but I never imagined anything like this. We all believed … well something … but when I saw you do *that* … it was like … turning the world upside down.' He took a sip from his tankard, and Art was sure he could see him visibly relax.

'Our people, Art, we're very different to you,' he continued. 'Our world is based on different ideas, different feelings, very rigid rules. If we don't live by those rules we can't concentrate, can't co-ordinate, can't do anything. When we're happy we unite in it, when we're not we unite to fix it, both sides, always working together. If we have different ideas that can't be resolved other than with the best manners, we accept it, separate and move on. We never call that wrong, just different. After seeing what I saw today, I think people here will have trouble accepting just how differently someone can live a life; I think they may eventually see it as wrong. And I'm not so sure they should have to make that decision.' He put his tankard down, and looked Art in the eyes. 'You can't blame yourself, Art. This isn't your doing. Our worlds are further apart than any of us took credit for, but this must stay between us. What happened on this mission *stays* on this mission.'

'But YerDichh's men, they were breaking the rules, they broke the protocol – you saw Scem's reaction,' Art said.

'I know, and that is disturbing enough in itself. The village will have a hard enough time accepting that without knowing what followed as well.'

122

Art thought of how he had seemed to instantly dislike Dabellar, and how the Fragment had blinded him from acting rationally.

'Could you read him?' he asked tentatively.

Sergeant looked at Art inquisitively.

'Shay-la told me. You don't look alike,' Art chuckled.

'I could,' Sergeant answered, 'but I didn't like what I saw. He was improvising, making it up as he went; it was hard to read, which is why I only knew he was going to use a Drop at the last second. But there was no remorse for his actions. It's never been done before, doing something the wrong way, without guilt. I don't know what it means, or what YerDichh is planning. It doesn't make sense.' He looked over at Scem, and Art could see the longing in his eyes to have his commander back. 'We need to get back to the village to try and make sense of this.' He tapped the side of Scem's tankard, and he and lifted it to his lips vacantly.

Art was starting to see what Shay-la meant about Sergeant; he alone had kept it together, taken the lead when his commander was down, willing to give himself completely to those above and below him to make sure everyone came home. Shay-la was an excellent fighter, Scem was an outstanding leader, but Sergeant was the glue that held everything together, and Art felt a fierce admiration for him, which made him feel even worse about how badly he had let them all down.

Sergeant made sure Scem and Shay-la had drained their tankards and then gathered all their thick coats in preparation for the short walk back to the village. Art was not looking forward to facing Hité, especially as she would know all about what had happened before he would have a chance to explain. Not that there was anything to explain. He looked down at the Fragment on his wrist that would keep him warm as he crunched through the snow and felt a rising resentment at its intervention. Why had this happened? Why had the Fragment given him the confidence to do something that seemed so right at the time but was so *very* wrong? Art was as confused now

123

as he had been when he first arrived at the village, and the thought of returning there now filled him with dread.

Chapter Eleven
Debrief

They walked through the snow for what seemed like ages, the air thick with falling flakes. Art couldn't see more than ten feet in front of him and had no idea whether or not they were heading in the right direction. Then, through the swirling snow, lights started to force their way through, and before long Art could make out a row of glowing windows, the brightest of which were coming from the house he had been given just before they left. Even now the thought of it seemed silly; he'd just been *given* a house – as if he was planning on staying here. It seemed a very strange land when he arrived, and just as he had started to get to know Scem and Shay-la and thought he was beginning to finally understand some of it, his own seemingly rational actions had made him realise just how little he really knew about these people, and suddenly he didn't fit in again, it was all alien, all strange, and none of it made sense any more. The big question that had puzzled him from the start was now burning brighter than ever: what exactly was this land and ... *where was he*? He was pretty sure he knew how he had got here – the Fragment had brought him. Only now was he starting to remember a shocked-looking Tina standing over his bed as he fought off an irresistible fatigue, but it wasn't a strong enough memory to fully believe yet, so he unconsciously dismissed it. Now his only thought was how he was going to get back; he would have to travel to the exact spot in the woods where he had woken with such a start the day before and hope it would get him home. If it didn't, he was in trouble.

Sergeant, who was still helping Scem and Shay-la to walk, suddenly stopped in his tracks and closed his eyes.

'Hité knows we're back,' he said.

This was just what Art had feared. 'So she knows what's happened then,' he said, a terrible feeling of dread building just above his stomach.

'No, I'll keep it hidden. Like I said, what happened out there stays out there.'

Art was surprised at this. He didn't understand how Mind-Charms did what they did, but it hadn't occurred to him that they could keep things from each other. All of a sudden he felt huge relief, like a heavy weight had been lifted off his shoulders. Sergeant smiled at him, a smile that could have been borrowed from Hité.

'Remember what I told you – it wasn't your fault, Art. Our only priority now is to try to make sense of what happened ... before...'

'...before I did what I did,' Art finished for him.

'Exactly.'

To Sergeant's surprise a flicker of life seemed to spark inside Scem, and he sat down, rubbing his face and head.

'Sir, are you okay?' Sergeant asked, and gently lowered Shay-la into a sitting position next to him.

She too was stirring, but was still very pale. It was as if being in the vicinity of the village was somehow healing them. Sergeant fished out a flask of water from his pack and helped Scem to drink from it. Art took it from him when he had finished and helped Shay-la do the same.

'I'm ... not so disorientated now, Sergeant, thank you,' Scem managed. He rubbed the back of his neck. 'What happened back there?'

A sharp pang of guilt erupted inside Art's chest; he hadn't thought for one moment that the shock would be bad enough to make Scem *forget* what had happened. He pictured having to tell Scem again what he had done, and he didn't relish the prospect.

'Don't worry about that now, sir, we all need to get inside for a debrief. It's not far.'

Art heard the sound of skis and two soldiers emerged out of the snow. Art recognised one of them as Corporal Pannett, who immediately looked concerned when she saw Scem and Shay-la sat on the ground.

'Sir, we'll get you back – don't worry about anything just now.' And they both unwound the fastenings of their worn wooden skis and rushed forward to help up their two seemingly injured friends.

Before long they were approaching the Horn Keeper Inn and darkness had started to fall. Art caught the familiar smell of Stroth-Brew, and could see the multicoloured light spilling out of the windows. He wondered why the smell was so much sweeter; then he realised he must have started a craze with his milk and honey. It hadn't really been his idea in the first place. Or had it?

Hité burst out of the large wooden doors and darted down the steps towards them. If Sergeant had kept what had really happened from her, he certainly hadn't withheld the fact that Scem and Shay-la were a little worse for wear. She rushed over, took Scem from Corporal Pannett's arms and ushered him inside, holding the doors open so that the soldier helping Shay-la could follow. She sat Scem down on the large sofa next to the fire and settled next to him, holding his hands. At first Art thought she was trying to read him, but then Scem started talking and looked quite alert.

'I'm okay, my love. Just a little shaken is all. We need to talk about … what happened; it's quite disturbing.' He threw a glance at Art, but had a spark of kindness in his eyes.

To Art's relief, and momentary horror, Scem seemed to have recovered all his memory, including Sergeant's instructions about what to withhold from the village. Art only now noticed that the Horn Keeper Inn was packed with villagers, all of them silent and staring at the returning party. There was a commotion from the back of the room, and Jonnoe pushed his way through and rushed to Shay-la's side, giving Art a scolding look as he passed. Shay-la just smiled at him.

'It's okay, Jonnoe, the Sta'an *knows* him. You should see … you should *see*…' she murmured in his ear, and slowly Jonnoe's face changed to a look of confusion, all anger gone.

Art didn't know whether she had also forgotten what had happened or whether she just didn't blame him, like Sergeant.

'We must hold a meeting,' Scem said quietly to Hité, and she nodded with a knowing look in her eyes.

'Leave it to me, love,' she said, and walked over to the edge of the fireplace where Art had noticed the rather small out-of-place panel of flashing lights the day before. She pressed a few of them in a seemingly random sequence and they beeped under her touch. She sat back down next to Scem, who nodded in Sergeant's direction. Sergeant fronted up to Art, looking business-like.

'Art, may we request the use of your residence for the debriefing? It requires a certain amount of privacy.' He nodded subtly towards the villagers.

'Oh. Er, of course,' Art replied.

'Then lead the way.'

Art felt useful again as he led them back out into the cold and down the frozen high street to what had previously been the Meeting Hall. There were lamps hanging from tall poles all the way down, making the scene look like a popular painting, and it gave Art a rush of excitement that he was here again, though he had no idea where the emotion came from. They reached the house and Art pushed open the huge doors. As he stepped inside, he realised he was doing so for the first time. The fire that had been burning in the grate that morning was still ablaze; someone had obviously been tending to it throughout the day. Scem and Hité followed him inside, then Shay-la and Jonnoe, and finally Sergeant. They all sat around the fire on the three huge sofas, except Sergeant, who fetched a pan of water and set it over the fire to boil, and before long there were six steaming tankards of Stroth-Brew on the table. Hité had brought two huge oven-warm loaves of bread with her

128

from the Inn, and they sat in silence eating and drinking, relishing in the refreshment of the simple meal. Art had had no idea he was so hungry, and finished off half a loaf on his own.

When they had all finished, Scem turned to business.

'Hité, I'm sure you are aware of where we were today.' He looked towards Sergeant, who nodded. 'But you may not be aware of *everything* that happened.'

Hité looked a little shocked; she and Sergeant had obviously never kept anything from each other before, and Art saw that she was a little hurt. Scem explained everything that had happened that day, including Art's use of Captain Mercian's Sta'an and the meeting with the Blue Triangle troops. When Scem told her that they had not fought fairly, she turned white and sat in silence for a while, trying to absorb what she had heard.

'I understand this is a shock. It's never happened before. We need to discover why it happened, which is why I called the meeting; we'll need Pud and Jimma's thoughts on this.'

Art was glad Scem had taken Sergeant's advice and hadn't told Hité the whole story.

'We know YerDichh is after the Portal, but breaking tradition to do it is very disturbing. We definitely need Pud and Jimma. But there's one more thing.' Scem gave Art a sympathetic look, then turned to Sergeant. 'I need you to show Hité *everything*.'

Art's insides twisted and he stared at Scem wide-eyed.

'You can't ... what happens... stays ...' Art stammered.

'I know what Sergeant said, and I agree with him, but Hité needs to know.'

Sergeant was also looking worried. 'Sir, I can't ... you saw how it affected Private Calsow and yourself, sir – she won't cope.'

'I understand your concerns, Sergeant, I really do, and I don't want to do it, but she must know.'

'Know what?' Hité interrupted.

129

She looked upset and frightened; it was the first time Art had seen her unsure of anything. He was dreading her knowing, dreading what she would think of him. The others had forgiven him, explaining it wasn't his fault, and although it was Hité who had tried to tell them all in the first place how different their two worlds could be, Art didn't want her to know she had been right. All these people had shown him since he arrived was kindness and a code of honour unlike anything he had seen before, and he was ashamed at what he had done. But he didn't resent Scem for wanting to tell Hité the whole truth; he had always faced up to his misgivings in the past, and he wasn't about to change now. He resigned himself to the fact that Hité, who had been so unreservedly kind to him, would soon know what he had done.

Scem looked at her with as much love in his eyes as he could muster.

'They betrayed our ways, which is unforgivable,' he said, 'but … we betrayed theirs too. And there will be consequences. I'm sorry to do this, but you must know the severity of what happened today so we can properly assess what might happen as a result.' He kissed her hands, then placed them in her twin brother's, who was sitting at the low table in front of her.

'Hité,' Sergeant said, 'you must see clearly what I'm showing you. Don't search, just let me show you.' And with that he closed his eyes.

Art saw Hité's expression turn slowly blank and her eyelids fell shut. Sergeant's face was calm, but after a few moments it twitched into pain periodically and his expressions were mirrored perfectly on Hité's own face. It was almost too much for Art to bear; he was sure that at any second she would go into shock, just as Shay-la and Scem had, and he could only hope she would cope with it as well as Sergeant.

Art watched as Sergeant shared his thoughts, the pair of them flinching and twitching. Eventually, Hité's eyes flew open and she broke hands with her brother with a sharp cry. She sat staring into space for a few moments, then blinked, took several deep breaths and made eye contact with Scem. He looked worried, almost frightened, and reached tentatively for her cheek.

'Are you ... how do you feel?' he said.

A sympathetic smile broke out across her face. 'I did try and warn you,' she said.

'I don't understand,' Scem replied.

'I've seen it before, silly,' she laughed. 'You're forgetting who greeted Captain Mercian when he arrived.'

Sergeant and Shay-la looked confused, but Scem showed a flicker of understanding.

'What do you mean?' Sergeant asked; now he was the one looking hurt.

Hité placed a hand on his and glanced in Art's direction.

'He's from *Art's* world. I couldn't quite believe what I was reading when he arrived, but his head was full of the worst things I have ever seen. I couldn't understand how he could harbour such thoughts at first, how he could stay sane with those things in there. But then I realised; they were all part of his daily life. Things that would seem inconceivable to us are just part of his day. Of course I wasn't seeing them *first-hand* like you.' She squeezed Sergeant's hand and gave Scem a kind smile. 'But once you've read a mind like that, you *never* forget.'

Shay-la looked down at her Sta'an inquisitively; she unsheathed it and stared at it, wondering how its twin could choose to obey a mind such as that. Jonnoe stared at it too as if he had never seen it before, his eyes full of excitement.

'I never knew, but ... it makes perfect sense,' he said, staring more closely. 'The way it knew Art, the things it could do. The things ... *you* can do,' he said, looking at Shay-la with adoring eyes.

She stared back at him blankly. 'What do you mean?' she asked, still slightly unsure.

'I think I know,' said Scem, his face alight with childish fascination. 'Shay-la, have you ever been Felled?'

'No one has ever had the chance, not even in training,' she said proudly, and rather quickly.

131

'And I bet no one *could*, even if they had the chance,' said Scem.

It took a while for Shay-la to absorb what he had said; she knew immediately what he was talking about, but couldn't quite believe it.

'I … can't be Felled either!'

'That's what I'm willing to bet,' Scem said.

Shay-la and Art stood up, and he withdrew the Sta'an from his sheath, which he immediately realised wasn't his. Sergeant handed him his Sta'an, which he had taken blindly from Shay-la a few hours before, and they swapped clumsily. Art handed her his Sta'an and she took it, staring at it intensely. She held them together, and Art remembered what she had told him about the two weapons.

'Do you really think?' she said.

Hité cleared her throat. 'As fascinating as this is, we're not getting anywhere. We still don't know why YerDichh's troops did what they did.'

'Yes, you're quite right, dear,' Scem said, as embarrassed as an adult caught playing with children's toys. 'It's still a mystery, but I wouldn't like to speculate as to why until we have Pud and Jimma's take on it. We've discussed all we can for now – I suggest we keep this strictly to ourselves until the meeting. Agreed?'

They all voiced their approval, and went about making sure they had the right Sta'ans before gathering themselves together to enter the curtain of snow outside. Sergeant was the first to head for the door, but Scem put a hand on his shoulder to stop him.

'Sergeant, you saved us all this evening. It's nothing less than I expect, but that doesn't mean I'm not grateful. *Thank you.*'

Sergeant smiled at his commander, closed his eyes momentarily making Hité smile at something unsaid but heard nonetheless, and walked out into the night. Shay-la and Jonnoe were next; Jonnoe was holding Shay-la tightly as they walked, and gave Art a look of kindness and renewed respect. Again, Scem stopped them momentarily.

'Private, your Sta'an was the quickest today, again. Keep it up. And Jonnoe, we'll need you again at the meeting. See you then.'

And they too walked out into the night with a smile for their commander. Now Art was alone with Scem and Hité. They sat back down and Hité refilled their tankards from the small pan over the fire. They sat listening to the crackle and hiss of the fire in comfortable silence, contemplating the day's events. Art could feel that Scem and Hité were deep in thought; he could see their eyes focused on nothing in particular, their breathing involuntary and slow. Art was wondering what they could be thinking about when he noticed Hité was holding Scem's hand very directly, leaving one hand free for their tankards, and that their expressions were flickering in perfect synchronisation – Hité *was* reading him this time, but they both had their eyes open. He had never seen that before; maybe it was something that required an unusually close relationship, and a lot of practice.

Despite the warmth and sound of the fire, something was making Art feel uncomfortable. He couldn't put his finger on exactly what, but he couldn't relax. He noticed out the corner of his eye that Scem and Hité had broken hand contact, and after a while Hité seemed to notice that something was bothering him.

'Is there something wrong?' she asked him.

He looked at her, wondering whether she knew what he was going to say and was just asking out of politeness. He wondered whether she could read him as easily as she could read Sergeant, or whether she would have to *look*, like she had that first night in the Horn Keeper. He was unsure, but his answer to her question seemed to find its way out easily.

'I miss home,' he said simply.

His answer surprised him too, and it wasn't until he heard himself say it that he realised just how much. He missed his faithful beagles, Speedy and Steph; he missed the conversations he and his brother had on a daily basis; he missed his room and his things; he missed his tools, and his yearning to make something made its presence felt like it had been there all along and

133

was resentful for being ignored. He also missed his parents, which was a strange feeling as they had always been there, and he'd never known what it was like not to have them around; he missed Peter, and Tina, and he missed someone else he couldn't recall, someone small, intelligent, elusive, and then, out of nowhere, the image of Evi hit him like a brick. It felt like an electric shock throwing him across the room, but he knew he was still sitting. He wondered why *this* memory had so forcefully pushed its way to the top, and that was when he felt the Fragment pulsing, vibrating through his very bones, clearing his mind, trying to tell him something. He looked down and saw it glowing very slightly, so that only he could see, and as it flashed in a way that somehow made sense to Art, a connection was made. Somehow, he knew right then and there that all he had to do was go back to the same place in the forest and think of the things he missed, and the Fragment would take him back. He knew he would have to *miss* them; just thinking of them would not be enough. He wasn't sure how he knew this, but he was remembering glimpses of putting the Fragment on his wrist for the very first time, and the feeling of helplessness as it invaded his mind. He remembered the way it had found his memories of Evi and how strongly it seemed to fixate on them, like she was the key to all of this. It seemed the memories of the people and things he missed would do collectively, but specifically *her* memory would be enough on its *own* to make the Fragment do whatever it did. It seemed silly, but then he realised he didn't miss her in the same way he missed his parents or his brother. It was that he missed being *able* to see her face, and the *possibility* of there being something between them was like a shining light inside him. Whatever that feeling was, Art knew that's all it would take to get him back. And for the first time since he arrived in this strange but wonderful land, he felt genuinely happy. He was going home.

By the look on Hité's face she had clearly noticed his mood shift for the better, and she also seemed to have guessed why.

'Art, you must give me one more day. Just one, that's all I ask.'

134

He gave her a quizzical look. 'But you've seen the trouble I've caused you all since I've been here – how can you possibly want me to stay?'

'Art, the only people who know what happened today have all just left this room, and they are sworn to secrecy; the rest of the villagers need to see you *properly*. Just take the day tomorrow to look around the village, talk to everyone, ask questions – I know you have lots of those. Just one more day, Art, please.'

Art thought hard for a moment; he thought about walking into the forest first thing in the morning and finding the spot where he had appeared, and imagining what he would find when he got back. He hadn't really thought about what would happen when he … well, *appeared* again, if that's what would happen, but now that he had he found some questions forming in his mind. Firstly, *when* would he get back? How many days had passed at home? Now that he thought about it the days did seem very short here. Secondly, *where* would he be? Until now he had just assumed that he would return to the same place he had disappeared from, but maybe he wouldn't. Maybe he would appear somewhere awkward, like in the middle of the street or a river, or a completely different *country*. How would he get out of *that*? And thirdly, if he *had* been gone a while, what would people be thinking? He was pretty sure that Tina had seen him disappear – the memory he had dismissed subconsciously earlier now seemed very real; would she have told anyone? Would they have called the police? He had no idea what he would be going back to, but he did realise something – thinking of going back, and of all the people and the things he missed back home, made him realise that a part of him would miss being *here*. The little lamp-lit street, the snow, the vibrant colours everywhere, even the people. The village had got inside him somehow, and he would miss it if it was gone. With another pulse from the Fragment, something suddenly occurred to him, like the last piece of the jigsaw puzzle – the feeling of missing the village would bring him *back*. He was inextricably connected to it via the Fragment, enough to take him in either direction.

He thought about Hité's request again, and with those revelations fresh in his brain he decided he *could* stay, just for one more day. For a start, he wasn't quite ready to face all the problems that might come with returning home, and he couldn't quite shake the feeling of missing the village if he left.

'Okay,' he said slowly, '*one* more day.'

A smile spread across Hité's face and she leant forward.

'Okay then. I suggest you start with next door.' She pointed to the far wall of the large sitting room. 'We'll see you in the morning.' And with that, she took Scem's hand and led him towards the door and out into the snow.

'Goodnight, Art,' Scem said just before he clicked the door shut.

'Goodnight,' Art said to himself, as he sat there on his own. He wondered what Hité had meant when she said to try next door, but the quiet and the heat of the fire had made his eyelids heavy, and he decided to wait until morning before he did any exploring.

He walked about the room blowing all the candles out in the brightly shining lamps and set about searching for a bedroom, if there was one. As it turned out, it was the first door he tried, a few feet to the right of the fireplace. He ventured inside and found a large elaborate iron bedstead with a mattress at least two feet thick covered in sheets and blankets, with two impossibly large pillows at the head. There was a dark wooden desk to the left, with a single candle burning in a simple candleholder, lighting the whole room surprisingly well. Some of the paintings on the wall showed him emerging from the Hut, just like those in the living room, and some with him standing next to the front door about to go inside. The frames were obviously freshly made; Art could tell this by their light colour and the smell of freshly carved wood mixed with oil from the paint, which was still drying and glistened slightly where it was thickest. Art knew instantly that the thought of missing this room alone would be enough for the Fragment to get him back. He instinctively headed for the huge bed, peeling off his clothes as he went, and sank into its unnaturally comfortable sheets, hearing the air

136

leave the mattress as he sunk further. Without a second thought he drifted off to sleep, leaving all his worries outside the door of his new room.

Chapter Twelve

The Artisan

Art woke with a start, the sunlight beating down on his head from the small window next to his bed. He sat up and rubbed his head. He had no idea what time it was, or even if it was still morning, but he felt incredibly well rested. He looked absent-mindedly at his wrist for his watch and there was the Fragment, still and silent, securely fastened with the leather twine. He pushed the blanket off his legs and swung them round to the floor. His clothes lay in a heap where he had pulled them off effortlessly the night before, but he didn't want to put the same ones on again; he'd travelled a lot and all he could think of right now was having a wash.

He ventured outside the room and found himself back in the huge drawing room. The fire was still glowing and the tankards were still on the table between the large chairs. To his left were two other doors. He had seen Sergeant go through the far one when he went to fetch the pan of water, so he tried the one nearest to him. Behind the door was a very simple room with wooden floors and plain white walls. There was a small metal bathtub filled with water with handles on each end, under a small frosted window. It was steaming ever so slightly. There was also a large white towel and a bar of white soap on the windowsill. *So someone has been in overnight,* he thought. They hadn't tended the fire or cleaned up the tankards, but they had prepared a bathtub for him. He wondered who this elusive person was – he didn't know whether to thank them or cover himself with the towel in case they were still there.

After cramming himself into the tiny bathtub and washing himself clean in the lukewarm water, he checked outside the door and then did a quick naked dash across the living room back into the bedroom. He checked the

138

top drawer of the chest of drawers and found clean sets of everything he needed. All pressed and folded neatly; doubtless the work of his elusive guest. He put on his boots, winding the long straps up to just below his knees, then secured his sheath back around his waist, with his, or rather Captain Mercian's, Sta'an snugly in place.

Art had no idea what to do next, so he walked blindly into the drawing room, hoping to find some inspiration there. Brilliant white light flooded in through the windows as the sun bounced off the snow outside and cascaded in wherever it could. He saw the tankards sitting on the table and suddenly felt a pang of hunger. It must be breakfast time. Art started to head towards what he thought must be the kitchen when there was a loud knock on the front door. He paced across the room and clicked open the latch. The door creaked open with an ear-splitting sound, and there, standing on the doorstep, was a very small boy dressed in tiny versions of adult clothes, complete with tiny bright-red leather boots with violet laces. He even had a tiny sheath around his waist containing what looked like a pencil. He was so tiny it would have been easy to mistake him for a newborn baby, except he was standing upright with his arms folded resolutely. Art had seen lots of these little children about the village, holding onto their parents' legs and looking at him cautiously. But not this child; he looked Art directly in the eyes, as if he was studying a diagram. Art thought he felt a glimmer of recognition; there was something about the eyes, and the nose. But it was impossible, and he dismissed it.

'Er, hello,' said Art after a short silence. 'Did you ... knock on my door?' he said incredulously. It didn't seem possible that this tiny person could have knocked as hard as that. The boy stared at him some more, then slowly opened his mouth to speak.

'So you're the big one then?' he said. His voice was impossibly high, but extremely well controlled.

'Well yes,' said Art.

139

'You're not very frightening actually. I didn't think you would be, and you're not,' he said matter-of-factly.

Art smiled ever so slightly. 'Well thank you, I try not to be,' he said.

'Your nostrils are very big, aren't they?' said the boy.

Art giggled. He supposed that from the little boy's position looking up at him, his nostrils would look kind of large.

'I suppose they are. Don't hate me for it, though,' he replied.

The boy thought for a little longer, then said, 'When you sneeze, I should think your bogies fly *everywhere*, don't they?'

Art was trying very hard not to laugh out loud now. The fact that any type of conversation, let alone such inquisitiveness, could come from someone so small seemed impossible.

'I hadn't really thought about it that much,' Art managed.

He thought the little boy must be getting very cold standing up to his ankles in snow, and was beginning to wonder where he had come from. He poked his head out of the doorway and looked up and down the street for signs of anyone who might be his parents or guardians, but the little lamp-lined street was completely deserted.

'Erm, do you live in one of these houses? Would you like me to take you home?' Art asked.

'No thank you. I'll just wait if it's alright,' the boy answered.

'Wait for what?' Art asked.

'Well, are you going to sneeze soon so I can see?'

Art almost laughed out loud this time.

'Er, I don't think so, no,' said Art.

The little boy looked peeved. Then he said, 'My brother says that if you pour pepper up someone's nose then they won't be able to stop sneezing for a whole morning.'

Once again Art stifled a laugh.

'And he told me,' the boy continued, 'that if you stick a pin in someone's bottom they'll fly to the moon.'

140

'I don't think anyone would be very happy with you if you tried that,' said Art.

The boy looked peeved again. Art made a mental note never to let this boy near a pepper pot or a sewing kit.

'You really should be getting home soon,' said Art. 'What's your name?'

The little boy screwed his mouth to one side, then replied, 'My mummy says I shouldn't tell strangers my name.'

'Oh,' said Art.

They stood in silence for a while.

'Well, it's Fallow,' the little boy said, 'but don't tell anyone I told you, or I'll *Fell* you.' He whipped out the pencil-like piece of wood from his sheath and waved it at Art menacingly.

Art could see now that the boy's Sta'an was actually an old paintbrush with the bristles pulled out. The sight of the little boy threatening someone at least ten times his size with no fear whatsoever made Art feel immediate affection for him. He was brave and clever for someone so young, and Art decided to play along. He moved his feet like he was trying to hold them still.

'No, please don't do that – I won't tell anyone, I promise,' Art feigned fear.

Fallow narrowed his eyes, then sheathed his weapon.

'Okay then, I won't,' he said, looking pleased with himself. 'Anyway, Daddy says you have to come over for some breakfast.'

'Oh, and where do you live?'

The tiny boy pointed to the door on his right; it was the house Hité had suggested he try first.

'In there; we're all waiting for you. And hurry up – I don't want to have to Fell you again.'

'Oh, absolutely not,' said Art, and hurried out into the snow, clicking his own door shut behind him.

He looked at the door of the next house; it had a symbol that looked like a hammer and chisel made into one tool very neatly carved into the door, and the familiar crossed Sta'ans symbol he recognised from Scem's hat just below it.

'Lead the way then,' Art said.

He reached down and the boy took his finger in his tiny hand, pulling Art through the crunchy snow. Fallow heaved open the door to his own house, which had been left slightly ajar so that he could get back in, and led Art inside. Art found himself in a drawing room roughly half the size of the one he had come from. To the left was a large round wooden table with five chairs around it, and to his surprise Jonnoe was seated in one; to his right was a little boy twice the size of Fallow with his head hidden behind a large leather-bound book. Jonnoe jumped up and rushed to greet Art.

'Good morning! I trust you slept well. Are you hungry?'

'Actually, yes,' said Art.

'Sit, sit.' Jonnoe ushered him towards the table and sat him in the chair next to his own.

Suddenly a door opened and Shay-la walked in carrying a large steaming pot of what smelled like porridge. Art was totally taken aback; she was dressed in a simple blue dress made of harsh-looking but free-flowing material, and her strawberry-blonde hair was loose and swept about her face as she walked. She was beautiful. Her soldier's uniform didn't do her looks justice at all.

'Good morning, Art,' she said with a smile. It reminded him of how he felt whenever Evi waltzed past him at school with a similar smile.

'Hello, Shay-la. Erm, thank you for asking me over.'

'Oh, it's nothing.' She placed the pot on the table and Jonnoe began ladling spoonfuls of porridge out into large, delicately carved wooden bowls.

Shay-la headed back out into the kitchen as Fallow jumped up into the seat next to Art. Art took a bowl from Jonnoe and placed it in front of his new tiny friend – Fallow flashed him a sly smile and began to eat clumsily from a large wooden spoon that looked like a garden shovel in his impossibly tiny hands. Shay-la returned from the kitchen with five mugs of Stroth-Brew and joined them all to eat. Fallow's older brother jumped down from his chair – his face still obscured by the book – and disappeared into the kitchen.

'So, Art, have you had a chance to look around the village yet?' Shay-la asked.

'Does news *always* travel this fast here?'

'Of course. My little boy is an excellent guide; he'll show you round after breakfast if you like.' She slid a little pot of honey towards Art, nodding to his bowl of porridge.

He added a little, stirred it around and tasted it. It was amazing; he didn't need to tell her – the look on his face said it all.

'It's not always that good, I'm afraid,' Jonnoe laughed. 'Just be glad you weren't here for breakfast yesterday when it was *my* turn to cook.'

Art remembered Hité telling him to ask questions –she had been right, he had plenty.

'Shay-la, tell me about the Portal. Where exactly *is* it?'

'Ah, straight to the tough ones. Hité warned me about this; I'll do the best I can.' She put her spoon down and picked up her tankard. 'There are some things you need to know about Portals before you can properly understand them. Firstly, natural Portals are extremely rare, which is not a bad thing. There are rumours of another Portal *inside* Hiro Mountain, but other than that the one here is the only one we know of. Secondly, they always lead off world; a Portal will never take you somewhere else *here*, only ... well, you know. And thirdly, part of whichever land they lead to spills out slightly between Portals. Apparently it was easy to spot this one.'

'How's that?' Art asked.

'Haven't you wondered why it's always cold and snowy here, in the village, when the rest of this land is warm and plush?'

'That's the *first* thing I noticed.'

143

'Well then, there's your answer.'

Art thought for a moment. 'So this Portal leads to somewhere … oh.'

Jonnoe laughed. 'All these clues and he still can't place this land.'

'Careful now,' Shay-la warned him, 'no pointers. You know the rules.' She turned back to Art. 'When the founders arrived here, they too were curious about the climate, and it wasn't long before they stumbled on its source. The Portal was right in the centre of the climate bubble, three feet below the ground. The Horn Keeper Inn was built over it to hide its existence; dangerous things, Portals. In the wrong hands, anyway. The rest of the village was just sort of built around it.'

'But if it leads somewhere cold, if it has a definite end,' Art said, 'how can it be a … what did you call it yesterday … a *positional* Portal?'

'A fully Positional Time Portal, yes. It has a *natural* opening, but it can be … shall we say *nudged* in a certain direction with the right know-how. A clever Mage can use one to go AnyTime-Where.'

'So it's underneath the Horn Keeper…' Art said to no one in particular.

Jonnoe cleared his throat. 'Of course, not everyone is privy to that information, Art. Many know it's here, but few know exactly *where*. It's safer that way.'

'I understand,' Art said. 'And what could happen if YerDichh got hold of it?'

Jonnoe shuddered. 'Who knows? Meddling with Time is never a good thing. The worst thing about it is that no one would ever know if it had been. Ever since the knowledge of Portals came out, people have thought they could use it to better themselves. But what few people ever realise is that if they ever managed to change it, make themselves richer or more powerful, they would never be aware of it. As far as they were concerned, their life would always have been that way. And what do people with wealth or power always want? More power, more wealth. They would try and change their life for the better again and again, never aware that they had done it even once.'

144

Art thought about this for minute; it made a surprising amount of sense to him.

'We have no idea what YerDichh wants it for,' Shay-la said, 'but whatever it is, it *can't* be good. We doubt he even understands that he'd never be aware of any changes.'

'A word of warning though, Art,' Jonnoe said, leaning closer to him and looking very serious. 'Going through a Portal, even once, as *you* have, brings with it certain risks. You'll only ever be aware of a shift if you happen to see someone out of time, or recognise someone who *has* been out of time. You should be prepared to see things you *know* are impossible. If you do, Time *has* been meddled with. Going through a Portal to its natural end brings no risk, but if you've been moved even one millisecond either way, be prepared. We have experts who know how to do it safely,' (Shay-la gave a grunt of disagreement) 'and do so on a regular basis, so it may just be the result of a calculated move, but it could just as easily be something very bad.' He moved even closer. 'If it happens, your first instinct *must* be to say *nothing*. Your second must be to think very carefully about what you eventually *will* say. Do you understand, Art?'

'Er, yes … yes,' he said, unsure at first.

Art hadn't thought he'd get such a detailed answer to the very first of his questions, or indeed such a stark warning, but in asking it he'd had quite a few others answered along the way.

'How do you know all this?' he asked.

'I'm the Village Carpenter – it's my *job* to know. I'm Scem's second-in-command.'

Shay-la smiled. 'Come on, we all know Hité's his second.'

'Well, his third then,' Jonnoe corrected.

'Then there's Sergeant.'

'Okay, fourth. You get the picture anyway.'

'The Village Carpenter … is that highly thought of?' Art asked.

Jonnoe looked momentarily offended.

145

'Oh, I'm sorry, I didn't mean to…' Art apologised.

'It's okay,' Shay-la reassured him. 'Arthur, this is a village of *Artisans*; we are all skilled in some form or another.' She placed a hand on Jonnoe's. 'But there is only ever *one* Carpenter in an Artisan Village. And he or she is the key to everything we do.'

'What *do* you all do?' he asked.

'Ah now, I can't tell you that.'

'Okay then, what does the Carpenter do?'

Shay-la smiled warmly. 'Take out your Sta'an and see for yourself.'

Art slid his Sta'an out of the sheath and held it with both hands. When he had first seen it he had marvelled at its workmanship, and now was no different. It was battle-worn, little chunks missing here and there, and a few light scratches, but the unbelievable craftsmanship was still clear.

'Each Sta'an calls to its owner when the time is right. It happens when the natural lifespan of a tree comes to an end; the last little spark of life hangs on in the last living piece of wood, calling to its natural owner. It takes a Carpenter to find that last living piece, and a great deal of skill to keep the spark of life inside it when crafting it into a Sta'an. Or whatever Charm belongs to the rightful owner,' Jonnoe explained.

He reached up into the neck of his tunic and pulled out a Charm on a leather twine to show Art. It was like a large wooden coin, with the same emblem as was carved on the front door and sealed with some kind of resin.

'A Sta'an is just a big Charm really; the only difference is that its powers extend beyond its physical form,' he continued, and put it back inside his tunic.

Art was awestruck. 'Wow,' he breathed.

'Of course, there's lots of other little jobs to do around the place,' Jonnoe said. 'You only have to look on the walls to see some of them.'

Shay-la was looking lovingly at Jonnoe. 'But you can see how an Artisan Village is literally nothing without its Carpenter,' she said.

146

Art was keen to know everything about Jonnoe's role here. 'So do you have a ... I don't know, a *workshop* or something?' he enquired.

Jonnoe's eyes lit up. 'Now you're talking,' he said.

Shay-la grinned. 'You've started something now. I'll clear the breakfast things away.'

'Oh, yes – thank you for that – it was delicious,' Art said.

Jonnoe rose from the table. 'Follow me,' he said, and led Art through a door next to the kitchen into a large room filled with natural light from skylights in the ceiling.

There were hand tools of every description hanging on the walls with an outline painted around every one, and an L-shaped worktop running along two of the walls. There was a rack of freshly cut wood of all types and in all shapes and sizes on the right-hand wall, and racks of fixings beside it. The worktops were spotlessly clean, as was the floor, but the whole room still smelled of sawdust and seasoning wood. It was the most amazing sight Art had ever seen, and he didn't know what to look at first; there were hand drills, saws, workhorses, chisels and even a foot-operated router. Every inch of wall was covered with tools, all incredibly well used and worn-looking, and all just itching to be used.

'Go ahead – have a look around,' Jonnoe said, looking very proud indeed.

Art walked over to the rack of wood and picked out a piece of mahogany, perfectly smooth, ready to be turned into anything by his hand.

'This place is amazing,' he said. He absent-mindedly wandered over to the worktop and picked a small handsaw off the wall. 'I just can't believe it!' He placed the wood over two of the workhorses, still gazing around at the wonderful sight, and automatically started cutting into the wood, sawing here and there, looking all around him as he did. 'I've never seen anything like it,' he said, as part of the wood fell to the floor in a shower of sawdust.

Jonnoe was staring at him with wide eyes.

Art was still incredulous. 'This is what you do, all day? Wow!'

147

Another piece fell to the floor, then another and another, and suddenly Art found he had no wood left to cut.

'Oh, erm, sorry, I … err … I do that sometimes.'

Jonnoe walked over to the little pile of wood, bent down and picked up four little chunks. He blew off the sawdust and there in his hands were four perfectly crafted little door wedges, all exactly the same size, in beautiful dark mahogany.

'Sorry,' Art repeated. 'I've got hundreds of them at home, they just sort of … pop out when I'm not thinking.'

Jonnoe was utterly speechless and he stared up at Art, who felt slightly uncomfortable.

'What?' Art said.

'You're a … you're a…'

'A what?'

'A Carpenter? The Scriptures were right, I mean … how *I* read them. *I* was right. I was … I don't believe it…'

'I wouldn't exactly call myself a carpenter, not really. I just like to make things with wood. It's just a hobby.'

But Jonnoe was insistent. 'No, no, no, look at these – don't you *see*? You can't *learn* that – *look* at them!'

Art thought about it for a moment. It was a bit hard to believe; how come Hité hadn't spotted it when she read him? Jonnoe rushed out of the room calling for Shay-la, brandishing the door wedges. Art followed him into the drawing room, where he saw the table had been cleared and Fallow was sat in a chair drawing with some charcoal. He heard a commotion in the kitchen and Shay-la rushed out holding one of the door wedges. Art was feeling quite embarrassed – they were only bits of wood after all, and he couldn't see what all the fuss was about.

'Did you make this?' she said, urgency in her voice.

Art felt silly owning up to making something so insignificant.

'Well yes, but…'

'Why didn't you say? Why didn't you *tell* us?' Shay-la was looking a little scary, like she had during their first battle lesson.

'I … I don't really know. I'm not a *carpenter*, they build *houses* and stuff. I just play with old wood and tools. What's going on? I don't really understand all this.'

Shay-la was staring at him, but Art was glad to see a hint of a smile at the corners of her mouth. The next thing he knew, she had stepped forward and embraced him as she had done before the attack the previous day. The thought of it made him remember what he had promised her.

'Hité must know,' she said, pulling away. 'I'll tell her. You must carry on with your day – nothing must get in the way of that.'

Art reached down to his sheath and withdrew his Sta'an. 'Well, I guess I don't need this any more. It should be back where it belongs.'

He handed it to Shay-la, who stared at it for a moment, then slowly reached out and took it. Art noticed a tear in her eyes. She cradled it in her arms like a baby for a moment, then reached round for her sheath, into which she carefully slid Captain Mercian's Sta'an next to her own. Somehow there was space for two, as if her sheath had been made that way.

'Thank you,' she whispered, and kissed Art's cheek. Then she composed herself, wiped her eyes and cleared her throat. 'My eldest son will take you round the village. He should be ready by now.'

Art heard a muffled voice from somewhere in the house. 'I'm *coming*, okay? Give me a minute.'

Shay-la rolled her eyes. 'Kids! Just wait outside, it's a beautiful day. He'll be right with you.'

Art thanked her again for breakfast and ventured back outside into the snow. Shay-la was right – the sun was still shining brightly, and Art loved the freshness of the cold as it filled his lungs. He looked up and down the street; there was still no sign of life, except the bizarre animal with the trunk-like arm in the distance, wandering the street alone, no longer bound to the

149

cart. Art heard the crunch of snow as Shay-la and Jonnoe's other son stepped out into the street and pulled the door shut behind him.

'Come on, er ... Art, isn't it? I haven't got all day.'

Art turned to look at him, and before he knew what was happening his legs gave way and he fell to the floor, staring in shock and disbelief. The feeling of recognition had stabbed him in the chest and he was struggling for breath. There, right in front of him, as surely as Art knew he had two arms and two legs, was a very young Maga.

Chapter Thirteen

The Battle

Art's heart was thumping in his chest. He sat on the floor in a state of shock, not quite understanding what was happening. But for some reason, Jonnoe's warning rushed to the top of his consciousness, and it was a good thing too. *Say NOTHING*.

'Whoa there – watch out for the ice. Let me help you up,' Maga said, walking over to him. He stretched out a little hand, but Art made no movement.

After a moment, Maga dropped his hand to his side and sat down on his haunches. 'Are you okay there? You look white as this snow.'

Say nothing, Art thought again. He stared into Maga's eyes – he was hoping to see something there that would persuade him that it wasn't Maga, some little sign that it could be someone else, but the sparkle in his eyes was unmistakable. Even the way he walked. This *was* his mysterious little 'sprite' of a friend who showed up every year, whom he laughed with, confided in, listened to and trusted with his life. Only now he looked a good two or three decades younger.

For some reason Art couldn't fathom, things that seemed unimportant in light of his state of shock started running through his head; for a start he now knew where the spark of recognition had come from when Fallow knocked on his door, and he also knew exactly where the Maga *he* knew got his feisty character from. Maga was *so* Shay-la's son it was frightening.

Inexplicably, the second part of Jonnoe's warning surfaced – *think carefully about what you will eventually say*. After all, he knew Maga well in this boy's *future*, but in his own *past*. His head was beginning to spin just thinking about it.

151

'Art? Should I get some help? Art?'

Art took a few deep breaths and tried his hardest to clear his head. *What should I say?* Needless to say this young version of Maga wouldn't know him at all, so he decided the best and easiest course of action was to act as if he was meeting him for the first time.

He extended a hand. 'Yeah, er … that was a bit of a fall. Didn't know where I was for a second there.' He rose to his feet; he towered above Maga, dwarfing him completely.

'Don't worry about it,' Maga said. 'It takes a good few years to get your snow-legs proper. I've been walking this street ever since I was born.'

He tapped the side of his head, as if pointing to that particular piece of knowledge, and Art reeled again at the recognition of the very Maga-like gesture. Maga sighed and attempted a small smile.

'I didn't introduce myself properly. I'm Maga.' He shook Art's hand. 'Sorry I was a bit short with you – I've got quite a lot to do today, and … well I suppose I was a *little* annoyed when Mum asked me to show you round the village.'

'Oh, listen, if you're busy I understand. You get back to your … whatever it is you've got to do.'

'No, no, it's okay. Besides, I want to keep an eye on you after that fall.'

'Yeah, my feet just slipped out from under me,' Art lied.

'I thought you were going to black out on me for a minute. Come on, we'll start this way.'

Maga led Art back in the direction of his own house. They passed his front door and soon Art found himself outside Dorin and Son's Fortified Wine Collectors.

'It's a bit too early to expect this place to be open,' Maga said. 'Dal-Seg only opens from about January to May, sometimes June if he's lucky. He's usually run out by then. But he's really busy when he *is* open, so you'd think he's open a bit earlier, wouldn't you?'

152

This was the first time Art had heard mention of the months of the year, and he liked the familiarity.

'Run out of what?' he asked.

Maga chuckled. 'Well fortified wine, of course. He only gets one batch a year.'

'Only one batch? Where does he get it from?'

Maga paused momentarily. 'Ah yes, Mum warned me about this – I'm not allowed to give you too many pointers. Let's just say there's a limited supply.'

'A *limited* supply? Limited by what?'

'Moving on,' Maga cut in quickly. 'Dal-Seg's brother, Wan-Seg, runs this shop,' he said as they passed the food and hardware shop. 'Dal-Seg helps out here when his shop's closed for the year. They sell the best Stroth-Brew in the land. Mind you, it's even better since you arrived. They're talking about putting up more shelves for all the milk and honey they need to get in. Jo'Sys in Trade Town loves *you* already.'

The windows were dark and draped with black curtains. The shop was deserted. Art wasn't used to seeing shops closed – even on a Sunday; his world suddenly seemed familiar and alien at the same time, always so busy, so driven, whilst this world was rife with tradition, fiercely so, and he loved it that tiny bit more for it.

Art looked up and down the street but could see no more shops, the rest of the buildings being little houses, all terraced, stretching to the end of the street. He counted thirty in all. They were all topped with snow and had streams of smoke running into the sky from their chimneys. To Art it was the most heart-warming sight he had ever seen.

Maga saw the look on Art's face. 'It is rather wonderful, isn't it? In the evenings the street is often filled with villagers just walking up and down, taking in the sight of their own village, cooling themselves down before they warm up again with a Stroth-Brew in the Horn Keeper. Stroth-Brew is always best taken when you're cold.'

Art noticed something strange about the way the buildings looked collectively. He couldn't quite put his finger on it, and he squinted in the hope it might help. Then it came to him. All the houses were brand new, with their perfect brickwork and immaculately painted exteriors, but they *appeared* ancient because of the angles of the walls and the sunken roofs.

'How *old* is this place, Maga?

'No one really knows, but Scem estimates it at five or six generations.'

Art had no idea of the length of time Maga was talking about, and the confusion showed on his face.

'Sorry,' Maga chuckled, 'about nine hundred years.'

Art did the maths in his head; that meant a generation was roughly a hundred and fifty years. Scem had been right when he called himself a young man at sixty-four.

'But everything looks so *new*,' Art marvelled.

'Oh, we like everything as it is – when things need replacing, that's exactly what we do, *replace* them, exactly as they were before. But come on – you haven't seen the best bits yet. Around the back of the village.'

Art could see the end of the street about forty or fifty yards up ahead. His attention turned to his newest *and* oldest friend.

'So you like it here then?' Art enquired.

'It's home,' Maga replied.

'I see Fallow is almost certain he's going to follow in his mother's footsteps. He nearly Felled me with his paintbrush this morning.'

Maga grinned. 'Yeah, he's known for a while. Some do; it's just natural from the start.' He sounded a touch envious.

'Oh,' said Art, 'and you don't? You honestly don't know what you'll be?'

'Well Mum and Dad think they know. They think I'll be a ... don't laugh, okay? They think I'll be a ... a Mage. Well Mum does, anyway – I think Dad just agrees with her for a quiet life. I haven't had any urges though; I still just feel like me.'

154

This made perfect sense to Art. The things he had seen Maga do in the four years he had known the much older Maga made him unable to imagine him being anything else. It certainly explained why Scem and Sergeant had heated water for Stroth-Brews using the fire rather than Maga's much quicker method.

'Why would I laugh at that?'

Maga gave him a thankful smile. 'Mages are very rare, and they're always *very* powerful. You don't really get mediocre Mages. They have to train for years, it doesn't just come naturally like when a soldier's Sta'an seeks him or her out or when someone comes of Charm age.'

'Okay,' Art said, 'but I still don't know why you thought I'd laugh.'

Maga looked embarrassed. 'Mum told a few people in the village about it and now most of my friends are laughing at me. They think it's impossible. The worst thing is I *agree* with them. I wish Mum would just shut up about it.'

Art wanted to tell him that his mother was right, that he would grow up to be one of the best. Well, the best he'd seen anyway. Actually the only one he'd seen, but amazing all the same. He didn't like seeing the young Maga suffer like this, but he was also wary of giving too much away, so he feigned ignorance.

'If I were you, I wouldn't worry about it. When the time comes and you know what you are, all your friends will see the true you. Until then, just laugh with them – don't let it get you down. Friends are very important, you know.'

Art had always known this, from as far back as he could remember. He could always rely on his family, but during the times when it *felt* that he couldn't, when his mother or father *knew* best but he was reluctant to admit it, his friends were always there for him. They would agree with the most ludicrous things he said, just for the sake of being supportive. And when he realised his family had been right, his friends would leave him alone with them, waiting in the background for when he needed them again. It was

155

natural, and he did the same for every one of his own friends, without even knowing it.

Maga didn't say anything, but Art could tell he was grateful he hadn't been given a lecture about always listening to his parents and he cheered up a little.

'Come on, just round here,' Maga said, grinning.

They had reached what Art thought was the end of the street, but he could now see that it didn't end here, and continued around the last house and back down behind the houses. He followed the road and realised that he had in fact seen less than *half* of the village during his time there.

There in front of him was a square lake, completely frozen over, surrounded by tall street lamps. Although still quite early in the morning, the lake was already half full of children and adults skating round and round, laughing and playing on the ice, chasing each other, some teaching, some learning, but all with glee on their faces. The street ran down one side along its length to the line of buildings at the end, giving the village its L-shape. Each of the little houses had its own enclosed back garden, with a gate that led out onto a verge before meeting the street, which had wooden benches of all sizes where people sat binding the rather primitive-looking ice boots to their feet with lengths of fabric. All the back gates were open, and people were wobbling along towards the natural rink, watching from the benches or bringing steaming tankards of Stroth-Brew out to their loved ones on the ice. The snow-covered street was *nothing* compared to this.

'Wow!' Art gasped.

Maga beamed. 'It's amazing, isn't it? We spend a lot of time here, skating, talking, catching up. We need it after the year's work.'

'*The year's work?*'

Maga slapped Art's back. 'You don't think we do this all year round, do you? We're on *holiday*.'

Art looked confused. 'On holiday from *what?*'

156

Maga wagged his finger at Art, just as Scem had done during his first battle lesson. 'Ah ah, no pointers, remember?'

Art noticed the buildings at the end of the road were taller than the houses and shops, and looked a little like one long building, a warehouse of some kind, but dark and deserted like the shops. It looked a little out of place.

'What goes on in there?' Art asked.

Maga chuckled. 'Sorry, no pointers, remember?' Maga could see Art was about to protest, so he changed the subject. 'So, the question is, do you skate?'

Art looked at the large rink and a childish smile spread across his face.

'I'll take that as a yes then. Come on!' Maga led Art down the road past all the little back fences, eventually stopping at what must have been his own back garden. He pushed open the gate and led Art into the little enclosure and then into a small snow-covered shed. Running along the length of the wall were several pairs of ice skates, all different sizes, on three huge shelves. Maga scanned the top shelf where the largest skates seemed to be and pulled a pair off. They were made of thick brown leather with very shiny blades, and two long pieces of fabric to wind around your leg and fasten them on with. Maga got a pair for himself too and they headed back out and across the road to the ice rink.

Art laughed at the ludicrous situation he found himself in; this morning he had woken up in a strange world for the third time and washed himself in the smallest, most uncomfortable bath ever, and now he was about to go ice skating. Could things get any more surreal? And far from having his questions answered, he now had a load more that no one *would* answer. What happened in the large building at the end of the village? Why was there a shop that only opened for half of the year? And what were these people on *holiday* from? But the most worrying of all, the question that felt heavy at the bottom of his stomach, was why was *Maga* here? According to Jonnoe it either meant Time had been meddled with, or it was *meant* to be

157

that way and had been changed for a reason. Which was it? Was there even a way to find out?

Maga and Art sat down on an empty bench and were about to start unfastening their boots when there was an ear-splitting sound. The Horn was blowing, as it had when Art first approached the village. It blew once, then again, then blew one long blast that lasted for several seconds. Everyone on the ice stopped dead in their tracks. Art turned to Maga, who had a slight hint of panic in his eyes.

'What does that *mean*, Maga?'

Maga swallowed and dropped his ice skates. 'It er ... well everyone knows what it means, it's just ... well we've never *heard* it before.'

'What does it mean?' Art asked again.

Maga looked at him. 'It means the village is ... well, under *attack*.'

After a moment the rink began to clear, with people plucking their children off the ice and hurrying back across the road through the back gates of their houses.

'Erm, we'd better get back inside,' Maga said, and they hurried through their own back gate, past the little shed and into the warmth of the house. They ran through the kitchen and back into the drawing room, where Fallow was still sat at the table, frowning at the furore.

'What's happening?' Fallow demanded, and jumped down from his chair pulling his little make-believe Sta'an from his sheath. He seemed to have Shay-la's natural battle confidence – in many ways he was even more feisty than Maga would grow up to be.

'It's okay, Fallow,' Art said, 'just stay here while we see what's happening, okay?'

Fallow frowned further still, but sat back down. He seemed to trust Art, and Maga looked surprised by how calm Art was.

The door to Jonnoe's workshop opened and Shay-la rushed through, looking anxious. She unsheathed Art's Sta'an and held it out to him.

158

'You'll need this,' she said. 'One person who can't be Felled is good. Two is better.'

'What's happening?' Art asked.

'Unsure. I need to join the troop, and fast. Maga, Fallow, you both stay *here*, understand?'

They both grunted an answer and Shay-la rushed out of the front door, Art hot on her tail.

At first it was difficult to see what was going on, as the sun was now blocked by a thick blanket of cloud and the air was heavy with snow. But in the distance Art could make out two distinct bodies of troops, one a small oblong three soldiers thick, the other a huge square five or six times the size, less organised, but fierce and relentless. With a heavy heart, he immediately recognised the discipline and order of the smaller troop as the L-Shaped Village's army. They were hopelessly outnumbered, but fighting well – they had already Felled the first complete rank of the Blue Triangle army without a single Fall of one of their own. Their Felling techniques were quick and sharp, each accompanied by a shout of explosive power as they focused every ounce of energy into the fight. They were clearly much better trained than YerDichh's army, whose blind fierceness left them open to the calmly aimed Sta'ans of Scem's troops. But then came the sound of a small mouth horn, blown sharply twice, and the Blue Triangle army split into three sections and set about trying to outflank their opponents.

'They need me,' Shay-la said, and she rushed out to join her troop.

Art watched her go, wondering what he could do, but then remembered what she had said: *two is better*. He rushed out to join her, unsheathing his Sta'an as he went. As he got closer, he could see the Blue Triangle army still splitting up into its sections, but as they moved, several were thrown into the air by their feet and ended up on their backs, staring up at the sky. They were not being careful as they went, and Scem's troops calmly picked off whomever they had a clear aim at. There was a sharp shout from within the village's army, before it too split up into three tiny sections, one led by

159

Sergeant, one by Corporal Pannett and the middle section led by Scem. His section was driving forward, trying to scatter their rival section, Blue Triangle troops flying momentarily into the air as they glided further towards their opponents. Sergeant was doing the same, but Corporal Pannett's troops were resting on one knee, aiming carefully at their rival section and making an impressive number of Fells. It looked to Art as if Scem's army was doing well, holding off and Felling soldiers left, right and centre, quite literally, but the truth was far more serious. Despite their best efforts, the Blue Triangles were just too large in number, and it wasn't long before their three sections came to rest and began aiming Fells of their own. With all the men they had lost, they still outnumbered Scem's troops by five to one, and even though they were slow and clumsy, their Fells soon began finding targets, and Scem's three small sections began to dwindle.

Shay-la ran towards Pannett's section and began Felling with her usual confidence and speed. She had tied her hair back and looked like the soldier Art had got on the wrong side of the day before; a few of the Blue Triangles recognised her and paid the price for their momentary lapse of concentration. Despite knowing she couldn't be Felled, she was fighting with concentration and confidence.

Art ran up beside her, but she saw him and shouted, 'Sergeant needs you – section three – hurry!'

And Art ran as fast as he could, feeling his feet wobble as Blue Triangles tried to Fell him, but to no avail. He arrived at Sergeant's section and stayed level with him, matching his speed and position.

'Glad you could make it, Elfee,' Sergeant smiled.

'Will Shay-la be okay?' Art shouted over the roar of the fight.

'Of course she will. As long as she's there and you're here, we have two sections that cannot succumb. And I seriously doubt they'll make short work of Scem's section.'

Sergeant aimed a few more Fells at the soldiers before him, and three went down in succession. The roar of the battle was lessening behind Art, and he turned round to see only three soldiers left standing, all with fierce concentration on their faces. He wished he could do what they did with their weapons, rather than just standing there, cluelessly immune to the Blue Triangle's attempts to take him.

'What do we do?' Art shouted.

'We carry on. It's all we can do. They won't take the village unless the battle is completely won, every soldier down. And that can't happen.'

Art looked round at the other sections, all as dangerously thin as Sergeant's. Even Scem's section was becoming weaker, and soon only ten of the village soldiers, including Art, Sergeant, Shay-la and Scem, were still in the battle, facing twenty troops or more *each*. They had regrouped into one last defiant section, Sta'ans raised, no hint of despair in the soldiers' eyes, though Art was breathless and scared.

Suddenly a voice boomed from behind them, a heavy, impossibly low cry layered with bass vibrations, which shook the very ground they were standing on.

'STOP!'

The Blue Triangle troops were enveloped in a strong wind that blew them off their feet as the cry continued, and they slid several feet on their backs, clinging onto their Sta'ans for dear life. Then it was gone as quickly as it had started, and the whole battlefield was still and silent. The remaining village army troops were still upright, though there was confusion on their faces. The Blue Triangles who had been blown over rose quickly to their feet, but were wary of restarting the battle. All eyes were on a solitary figure somewhere behind Scem's remaining soldiers. Shay-la turned around, and standing just behind her was Maga, looking angry and shocked, the air around him shimmering.

The silence continued for what seemed like an age, but was finally broken by a strong commanding voice in the distance from behind the Blue Triangle army.

'So, you have a Mage. I thought as much.'

161

Chapter Fourteen
Stalemate

Shay-la couldn't help but beam with pride at her son, standing there having halted the battle by a means that had even taken *him* totally by surprise. Even Art was smiling, now that there seemed little doubt Maga was indeed a Mage.

The Blue Triangle army's lead section slowly parted and Art saw a slightly built figure walking through them towards what was left of Scem's army. He was flanked by two figures, both of whom Art had met before: Dabellar and the un-named man who had outwitted three of the village's best soldiers, including its commander, before Art had made his big mistake. It was obvious to Art that Dabellar was a Mage too, a connection he hadn't made until now. If the Maga he knew *was* a Mage, Dabellar was the only other person he had seen use the little stopper-bottles for the amazing feats Art had witnessed. Art could see his Sta'an in the sheath around his waist and wondered whether he could really use it or if it was only there to hide his true skill.

The three men came to a halt a few feet away from Scem, who had walked out to meet them. Art assumed the slim man was YerDichh, who he knew was the leader of the Blue Triangle army. He was slightly shorter than Art, but still towered above the rest of his men, including Dabellar. He didn't immediately strike Art as being very old, but he could see the tiredness in his eyes, and the appearance of very fine wrinkles around his forehead and mouth. He had blonde hair, his cheeks were flecked with freckles, and his eyes were large, almost out of proportion for an adult even of this world. He didn't look like the menacing character they had all described, even in

162

comparison to Dabellar, who was standing just behind YerDichh's right shoulder, glaring at Art with a mixture of hatred and fear. His left eye was black and swollen, and Art felt another stab of guilt in his chest.

'Not very sporting of you to *hide* a Mage in your ranks, Commander. You have already met mine of course.' YerDichh gestured towards Dabellar, who bowed reluctantly. YerDichh's voice was high, but strong and layered with false politeness. He seemed to command respect very easily; he had control over a huge army, led by a very powerful Mage, all of whom seemed happy to follow him into battle.

Scem's face had the hint of a smile, subtly victorious. 'Nice to finally meet you, YerDichh. To be fair, I must point out that Maga has only recently shown us his power. Though I'm rather glad he did.'

YerDichh's mouth curled into a false smile. 'Well, what a position we are in. Shall we discuss the terms of this stalemate? Or shall we pit our magicians against each other?' He raised one eyebrow as he spoke.

Dabellar glared at Maga, who was gaining some composure, and then stared back at YerDichh with calm contempt.

'I'm sure you don't want to do that,' Scem replied. 'I may decide to play my Joker.'

YerDichh narrowed his eyes. 'Your Joker?' he asked.

Scem smiled broadly. 'May I introduce Arthur?' He gestured towards Art, who copied Dabellar's bow but with relish.

YerDichh eyed Art with fascination.

'Though we deeply regret what happened,' Scem continued, 'an incident which will *never* happen again, I'm sure you have heard by now of his … shall we say *unique* talent?' It sounded as though Scem was exaggerating Art's power – all he could really do was stand there and not be Felled. Hardly anything spectacular. But whatever he was doing, he seemed to be playing his cards close to his chest; either he was keeping Shay-la's similar talent withheld for now, or he was still unsure of it. It was still just a theory after all.

163

'Ah yes. Arthur. I have heard of you. I am *very* pleased to meet you,' said YerDichh, still with a sickly smile drawn across his face.

'Likewise,' Art said simply.

'However, Commander, I still require the immediate surrender of your Portal, including all of your knowledge pertaining to it.'

'*Not* happening,' Scem said, 'and I seem to remember telling your men as much yesterday. Why do you think my answer will have changed?'

YerDichh rolled his eyes. 'I had hoped you would reconsider. Shall we call it a *request* this time?'

Scem suddenly looked angry. 'You think waging a *war* on my village is any way to make a *request*?'

'You think *assaulting* one of my men is any way to *deny* a request?' YerDichh spat back.

There was a gasp from the soldiers on both sides, and Art closed his eyes as if trying not to remember.

Scem took a deep breath and calmed himself. 'You have a point,' he said.

Art suddenly felt very small; this whole mess, this whole *battle*, was his fault and everyone knew it.

'However,' Scem continued, 'may I also point out that despite the severity of our ... misdeed, your Mage introduced himself as a mere soldier. *You* broke protocol first, then used your Mage to try and take the battle from us.' Scem's anger was rising. 'Such deceptive techniques have *never* been used before, YerDichh. NEVER! How can anything be more important than our respect for each other? Our Founders split into separate settlements on the understanding that our differences were to be *celebrated, honoured, respected* – we cannot fail them on that! We MUST stay true to ourselves.'

'But I DON'T BELONG!' YerDichh blurted out, then wished he hadn't.

Dabellar's expression faltered and he looked angrily at his superior.

YerDichh straightened up. 'I NEED THAT PORTAL!' he shouted. 'I *will* take this village by force if I have to!'

Dabellar's grimace returned and he focused his glare back on Maga.

'Look around you,' Scem said calmly. 'You cannot win a battle unless the field is levelled completely in your favour.' He looked towards Art. 'And I don't think that will happen. Unless you plan on breaking that rule too.'

Just then Scem felt a hand in his and turned to find Hité next to him. He went to protest, but she put a finger to his lips and he fell silent. She had a melancholy look in her eyes. She turned to YerDichh.

'Hello, Danny,' she said.

He turned white as a sheet. There was a long silence as YerDichh and Hité stared at each other.

He eventually stuttered a response. 'N ... no one's called ... that was...'

'Forty years ago, yes,' Hité replied. 'And you still haven't found your way home. You've lost your way in more ways than one.'

He stood in silence, trying to process what was happening. Then he shook his head and rubbed his eyes. 'No ... no, I *need* that Portal. You WILL give it to me...'

'You *don't* need it,' Hité cut him off. 'You never have.'

Now Scem was looking confused. 'What is going on, Hité?'

'I don't fully understand myself yet,' she said. 'I caught little glimpses as soon as the battle came to a halt, but it's buried very deeply, and a lot of past is in the way. But I will understand, if ... if you'll let me, YerDichh.' She held out both her hands to him. 'May I?'

YerDichh looked hesitant, reluctant, bordering on angry. 'And what exactly will you be looking for?' he said.

'Simply what you've forgotten, Danny.' Her use of that name again seemed to stir something in him, and his eyes looked a little softer. 'You can see them again, but you must *want* to.'

He looked confused and almost frightened, but slowly his shoulders fell and he relented. He stepped forward, ready to take her hands.

'What are you *doing*, sir?' Dabellar whispered as loudly as he could.

'Are you *questioning* my leadership, Mage?' YerDichh spat back. Dabellar

165

faltered, but reluctantly fell back in line.

'Of course not, sir. Just – watch the girl. She's dangerous.'

'I can handle the girl,' he called over his shoulder, then reluctantly gave his hands to Hité. 'I need my consciousness, mind-reader,' he hissed.

'I'll do my best,' she replied. She closed her eyes and Art could see that YerDichh was battling to keep his open, but he was obviously strong and stayed alert.

Hité's face flittered between expressions while YerDichh fought to keep his still, and doing surprisingly well. Hité slowly became breathless with concentration and her face contorted into an unreadable mixture of thought and strength. Then, with a sudden gasp, she broke hands and her eyes opened. She looked at YerDichh with pity in her eyes.

'I … I had no idea … but … you were *seven*,' she whispered, 'just seven.'

He looked at her with confusion. 'That makes no difference,' he said, 'I still need that Portal.'

'No,' she said, 'it's been so long you're confused as to what you need. You don't need to control our Portal, you just need to get *back home*.'

YerDichh looked vacant, empty, as if something was surfacing in his mind, and then his eyes glazed over and became filled with longing.

Scem's eyes widened. 'You don't mean…'

'That's exactly what I mean,' Hité said.

Art was being left behind. 'What are you talking about?' he said.

Hité turned to him. 'This may be good for you to hear as well, Art. You see, our worlds are so very different. Being here or being there doesn't affect us on a conscious level, but for some unknown reason, Pud and Jimma believe it's something to do with our laws of physics clashing with yours, visitors from your world don't *age* here. For some reason, our Time just doesn't seem to affect you. And vice versa.'

Art looked at YerDichh, who was still locked in thought. 'But he's not … he can't be. *Look* at him – he's … well, he's *small*, like the people here, but he doesn't look … young,' he said tentatively, unable to think of a polite way to say it.

Hité smiled warmly. 'Look again,' she said.

Art looked deep into YerDichh's face. He saw that his skin was covered in thin age lines, and his expressions and mannerisms were not those of a child. But as Art squinted, he began to suspect that he wasn't one of the people from this strange world after all. There was something about his face; it was too … human. But it didn't make any sense; leading an entire army into battle and commanding the respect of so many soldiers certainly wasn't the behaviour of a child. Art was struggling with the concept.

'I don't understand,' he managed.

Hité placed a hand on his shoulder. 'His body hasn't grown up, but his mind *has*,' she said, like it was the most natural thing in the world. 'Time can halt *physical* growth, but nothing can stop the mental development of the brain. It grows with *experience*, not Time.'

Shay-la sheathed her Sta'an. 'Remember what I told you about Portals, Art. They are rare, and unpredictable. And sometimes they can shift momentarily on their own. When that happens, someone can pass through unexpectedly. I'm guessing that's what happened to Yer … *Danny*.'

Hité put her hand to her forehead, as if she had remembered something that had been staring her in the face all along. 'I don't believe it,' she said, 'why didn't I *see* it…?'

'See what?' Art asked.

'The Scriptures were right. They mentioned your second coming, but were very vague about your *first*. *This* is why you're here, Arthur – there is a lost soul who has to get back. Someone who doesn't belong.' She looked at the temporarily incapacitated leader of the huge army in front of them. '*Danny*.'

YerDichh stirred, but his eyes were still focusing on nothing. Then he spoke, but his voice sounded different, as if he was somebody else; less commanding, and a little scared.

167

'I just went downstairs. I wanted to see what was left. I thought I heard a noise and it scared me, and I just … ran at it in fear. Fight or flight – at that moment I chose *fight*. And there was a flash of light, and I was lying in the dark, in a big wood. I was scared and cold, and I crawled blindly until it got light. And … I remember seeing two huge mountains, and sunlight, then … I was found and brought here…'

Art still couldn't believe what he was hearing. 'You were *seven*? Only *seven*? And you've been here for four *decades*?'

YerDichh focused on Art. 'I just wanted my … my parents. That's all I wanted. Just to *see* them, just once more…'

'That doesn't sound like an unexpected shift to me,' Scem said. 'It sounds like you were caught up in the tail-end of a planned trip.'

Hité took YerDichh's hands again. 'Danny, listen to me. *Our* Portal won't take you back to your parents, it doesn't work that way. But there's…'

'IT WILL! IT HAS TO!' He was starting to sound like the seven-year-old boy he really was.

'I hadn't finished,' Hité said calmly. 'BUT, there are some people who *can* get you back.'

Danny stared at her with a sudden spark of hope; then his eyes darted towards Art, who
looked like a rabbit caught in a car's headlights.

'No, no … I mean … what can I do? I have no idea what to…'

'No, Art, your part is done. Just your *presence* was enough. It drew him to you.'

'That's right!' Danny blurted out. 'When I heard of you, I sort of knew you were from home. I just *knew* it. I *had* to come.'

'Yes, but you didn't have to start a *war*,' Scem said angrily.

That seemed to bring everyone back down to earth with a bump.

'Oh. Yes, I'm sorry about that,' he said sheepishly. Then all of a sudden, his feet flew into the air and he crashed down onto his back.

168

Shay-la drew her Sta'an again and braced herself for battle once more. The un-named man had Felled Danny by Dabellar's command.

'You're *sorry*?' Dabellar spat as he finally bubbled over with anger. 'You're SORRY? You promised me full access to the Portal! A few heart-warming words from this lot and you're crumbling? Your years of promises and training amount to this? TRAITOR! I don't know how you did that, Mind-Charm, but you'll regret it. My strength of mind over anyone has never been broken.' He raised his arm and his remaining troops readied their weapons.

Scem's few remaining soldiers did the same, though it seemed there was little hope of victory.

'What are you *doing*?' Scem asked angrily.

'If this weak-minded buffoon isn't up to the job, then I will finish it. The Portal will be mine, even without his knowledge. I'll find it and I will master its secrets.'

'But the battle can't be won – you've seen that, first-hand.'

'You stick to these pathetic *rules* like a religion! When I first met YerDichh I couldn't believe there was another way. I was shocked at first, but when I saw what could be accomplished – stick to the rules? It's laughable now. I was sure he could lead these pathetic village soldiers to victory – it didn't take me long to make him my unwary slave. But I was wrong. And this will not stop me!'

'I think you'll find,' said Hité, 'that Danny was actually too *strong* to stay under your control, not weak at all.' She smiled in Danny's direction.

'SILENCE! RELENT!' Dabellar shouted, and pulled a long staff from his sheath which glowed with a fluorescent light.

Scem's eyes widened in fear.

Danny jumped to his feet, very rudely, and fronted up to Dabellar. 'How *dare* you disobey me?' Danny said venomously. 'YOU WILL STAND DOWN THE TROOPS AT ONCE! THIS IS OVER!'

'Ah, now then, I don't think that will happen. It's a consequence of the controlling process you see; they will only answer to me. They are ...' he sneered at Hité, '... much *weaker* than you.' He held his staff aloft and all of his fallen troops stood up at once.

His army was complete again and stood ready to fight. There were gasps from Scem's remaining soldiers, even the Felled ones, who were propping themselves up on their elbows so they could see what was going on. The whole situation seemed a bit bizarre to Art at that moment, watching the soldiers who were out of the battle lying there, unharmed, but unable to fight any more.

'And *you* answer to *me!*' Danny hissed.

'Do you really think you've been in charge all this time? Haven't you been listening? *Really?* You were a way to get to the Portal, nothing more. Your association with this village interested me, and your willingness to do things differently was so intriguing I let you have your little war games. But no more – you had your uses, you showed us the way, but you have failed; I will not. Now stand aside, or join the losing team.'

Danny looked outraged. 'But they can get me *home* – that's all I wanted!'

'Then you shouldn't have come to *me*.'

They stared at each other, fuming.

Scem interrupted. 'Erm, sorry to trouble you, but … can you hear that?'

'Hear what?' said Dabellar irritably.

There was a faint rumble under their feet. At first, Art though the battle was recommencing, but this rumble was different, intermittent, not like the constant roll of an attempted Fell. It grew louder, and Art heard the faint sound of cheering behind them back at the village. He turned round and from out of the falling snow the outline of the huge cart-beast appeared, running hard with a look of pure rage in its eyes.

Scem smiled his victorious smile. 'Zurioa doesn't look very happy. She's very protective of her village.'

170

Art could see the fear in Dabellar's face now. The beast was closing in fast and the Blue Triangle troops were starting to scatter in confusion.

'I really wouldn't be here when she arrives if I were you,' Scem said casually. 'Not even your staff will save you, but I'm sure you know that.'

Dabellar's face was contorted with rage. His staff glowed brighter than ever, and Art was glad that he didn't have time to use it as he didn't want to find out what it could do. Dabellar screamed in sheer anger and turned on his feet.

'THIS IS NOT OVER!' he shouted over his shoulder.

'Yes it is,' Scem replied, and watched as the Blue Triangle army fled in panic.

As Dabellar disappeared into the blanket of snow, Art had the feeling that it wasn't over, that he'd be back. For some reason Dabellar wanted the Portal badly, and he didn't seem like the sort of person who would give up so easily.

The beast finally arrived behind them and came to a halt, steam pouring from its huge nostrils with each breath. She sidled up to Scem and wrapped her trunk-like arm around his torso. He patted her, reassuringly.

'Well done, Zu-ey. Good girl.'

She whinnied appreciatively, still with a spark of anger in her eyes at the fleeing army.

Art wasn't quite getting this latest turn of events in the battle. Everyone had worked so hard to make sure no one was actually *hurt* during this battle, and things had become pretty awkward when it looked like Dabellar was going to break those rules. But now this huge threatening creature had ended the battle by causing fear and panic, and Scem and his army hadn't batted an eyelid.

'Surely *that* can't be playing fair,' Art said, now that the Blue Triangles were out of earshot.

Scem gave him a sideways look. 'What do you mean?'

'Well, the panic on those soldiers' faces, and Dabellar's...'

171

'Oh I see,' Scem said, smiling. 'No, Zurioa is quite a unique beast. She has the most noxious scent glands that will make you vomit for a week if you get hit by it. It's quite harmless, I assure you. Relax, Arthur, you did well. Enjoy the victory.'

Art was dumbfounded. He had been chastised for his moment of physical contact in battle, but what had just happened was nothing short of chemical warfare, and it seemed perfectly acceptable. Maybe he *did* have something to teach them after all.

Scem raised his Sta'an high into the air, and all of the Fallen soldiers rose to their feet and brushed themselves off. Then a great cheer erupted throughout the ranks and they all linked arms in celebration. The sound was deafening, and Art couldn't help but smile as Scem, Hité, Sergeant and Shay-la all surrounded Zurioa and patted her enormous shoulders, cheering as loudly as everyone else. Even Danny was cheering, looking incredibly like the child who had strayed into this world so long ago, desperate to get back, so very lost in so many ways, now hopeful that he could be forgiven, even helped.

Art looked round at the cheering soldiers and immediately spotted Maga standing in the same spot, looking more shocked than happy. He was smiling, but it was obviously forced. Shay-la spotted him too and ran over, embracing him in a vice-like grip as if to hold him in place. Maga didn't react at all. He just stood there being crushed and his face fell to a look of disappointment.

'Oh well,' he said, 'I guess my training will start soon.'

Shay-la held him at arm's length. There were tears in her eyes.

'You bet it does. Just look what you did! You were amazing – and they'll spot that straight away, you mark my words!'

They all gathered together and started to head back to the warmth of the village, all except the recently rediscovered Danny, who stood there looking very nervous and wondering whether he should follow. Art felt sorry for him; he had been there so long he had as good as forgotten who he was until

Hité had helped him remember. To the very small funny-looking people here, Danny probably looked just like a normal young man, and he was probably treated as such; all the things he had done, the things that had made him notorious in this world, had been done out of desperation to get home, and a little controlling magic from his 'subordinate'. But he had even forgotten that *home* was what he was looking for, and he had lost his way. A seven-year-old boy lost in a world where he was treated like an adult – it wasn't surprising he had turned out as he had. Art suspected that Danny had a lot of explaining to do, and he was looking forward to hearing it.

Hité turned round, sensing Danny's reticence. She walked up beside him with a warm smile on her face and linked arms with him, leading him on.

Art caught up with Maga walking arm in arm with his mother, who was chatting excitedly about his training and giving him little hugs every now and then.

'You don't look very happy about this, Maga,' said Art.

'Oh go on,' Shay-la answered for him, 'no one ever *knows* they're going to be a Mage. Some of them don't even *want* to be. But it's an honour, let me tell you. No technology, just natural magic; that's how it should be.'

Maga was still looking over-awed by it all, but Art was sure a good tankard of Stroth-Brew would put him right. He was amazed to find that he was looking forward to a few cups of the stuff himself, and couldn't think of anything else he wanted more right then than to sit in front of a roaring fire and drink, absorbing the chatter of the villagers around him.

Dialogue Three

'*Jimma. We have a red flash. What should I do?*'

'*A what? Really?*'

'*Yes, really. We haven't had one before. Not on this console anyway. What's the protocol?*'

'*Good question. Let's analyse it first, then we'll decide what to do. Where is it?*'

'*Secondary sector. Almost bang in the middle of it. Looks like a pretty powerful burst.*'

'*What's the source?*'

'*Well, the signature looks organic, but that can't be right. You don't get that kind of power from anything non-technological. I'll run a diagnostic on the sensors.*'

'*Okay, let me know when it's done. I'll be...*'

'*It's through. All seems fine.*'

'*Wow, that was quick! I didn't think the console was that fast.*'

'*It is now – I updated the files and replaced the processor. Your uncle's memoirs are an interesting read. Do you know he found the blueprint for the original processor on the underside of a water lily? Obviously it was just a random pattern, but somehow, among the veins and natural lines, he spotted the basic layout that enabled a processor to deal with multi-linear data – he just needed to join a couple of the dots and there it was.*'

'*Interesting. Honestly. Shall we get back to the matter at hand?*'

'*Sorry, yes. I'll run the linear-cams back a few minutes and see if we can simulate another reading of the anomaly. Okay, two should do it, and ... running. Now we wait till it picks it up again.*'

'*Okay, good. What will that tell us, Pud?*'

'Well, it will confirm if it was a genuine reading and not a malfunction, and we'll be able to see the radius of effect first-hand on the terrain scale. Should be any second now ... there it is. Whoa! That's a strong one. That can't be organic. And look at how far out it reaches – nearly half a mile! What does it mean, Jimma?'

'I'm not sure yet. First of all we need to get the correct protocols. The envelopes are in the safe here – just punching in the code – look away please, Pud.'

'Oh for Heaven's sake. Do you want me to turn around again?'

'That's enough, Pud. You know what happened last time.'

'What? Nothing happened last time. I think that reprimand was more in your head than anything.'

'JUST LOOK AWAY, WILL YOU?'

'Whoa there ... okay, okay. Looking away. Still looking away. Looking away, still happeni...'

'I'M WARNING YOU! That's better. Okay, the door's open. Here it is – the red envelope. Now then ... procedure for reporting a red flash ... Pud, was the reading stronger than thirty "Jimmas"?'

'Thirty what? I can't believe you're bringing this up again – you did NOT invent that unit of measurement. It's a joule. You mean a joule.'

'It's clearly documented in my uncle's memoirs. He was thinking of me when he fell into that swamp and came up with the idea.'

'Oh for ... whatever.'

'Well, was it?'

'Was it what?'

'Stronger than thirty "Jimmas"?'

'I'll say it was.'

'How strong was it?'

'Seventy-four.'

'Seve... Are you sure?'

'Absolutely. I told you it was a strong one – that's nearly three quarters of a "Pud".'

'I'll ignore that. Well, the protocols for any red flash require a report up the chain, but according to this, anything stronger than thirty "Jimmas" must be logged as an incorrect reading and reported directly to the Boss.'

'Wow! That's two Uniform Red connection requests in less than a week. Will my access codes do again?'

'Absolutely. Patch it through.'

'Headset again?'

'Not this time, Pud. I think I'll need you on this – you are our resident expert on Nature Versus Tech after all. Listen in, and contribute as much as you can.'

'Wow! I didn't know you cared. Honestly I didn't.'

'I don't. Now get on with it.'

'Okay, coming online – connection requested ... processing ... taking a bit longer this time ... still pro... There it is. Patching through to main speaker.'

'Boss here.'

'Morning, sir. Sorry to trouble you on your holiday, but we have a red flash to report.'

'Which sector?'

'Second, sir. I'm a bit worried about this one – Pud thinks it can't be organic, and it's way too strong to be any of the tech currently in existence. We could be looking at a rogue entry through an unknown Portal – it certainly didn't come through ours.'

'Okay. Pud, talk me through it.'

'Morning, sir. Well it flashed up just a few minutes ago just off-centre of Sector Two, and it hit big, real big, sir. The console reads it as seventy-four JOULES, with a radius of just over half a mile.'

'Seventy-four? Are you absolutely sure of that, Pud?'

'Yes, sir – we ran a simulation of the exact event again for confirmation. That's three quarters of the power it takes to open a Portal, sir. We have no portable tech capable of that, and needless to say it can't be organic in origin.'

'Ha-ha, well I never! The L-Shaped Village has its first Mage! I'll inform the Instructors immediately!'

'Sorry, sir, did you say a Mage?'

'Yes! This is excellent news!'

'Sir, that can't be right. Nothing organic, not even an accomplished Mage, can generate anywhere near that kind of power.'

'Ah well, you see this is no ordinary Mage. You may want to prepare yourself for this. He's a Founder.'

'................'

'Oh my... Sir, did you just...'

'Yes, Jimma, I said Founder. It's been documented since the beginning that one of the Founders was born out of Time, and that we'd know by the seemingly impossible power he displays that it's him. Or her – there's nothing on the Mage's identity. The Instructors will know what to do.'

'Erm, well okay then. Is there anything Pud and I can do, sir?'

'As a matter of fact, yes. It's been bought to my attention that little Daniel has been located. Sorry I had to keep you in the dark, but that was the reason for Arthur's trip here. It's time for them to be returned. Be careful though – I don't think it's a coincidence that these two things happened at once; this whole thing may be bigger than any of us. The Fragment found Arthur for a reason after all – we certainly had nothing to do with that. And we still can't be absolutely sure who sent him through – I know we were planning to anyway, but there's still some confusion as to whether us hitting the button actually did anything. You two seemed surprised when he appeared in the Portal that's for sure - I know that the nature of our job means the effects of things don't always happen in a linear sequence, but we still can't be absolutely certain.

Anyway - Danny came through on the tail end of a training exercise that went wrong. You'll spot the anomaly as soon as you scan the logs. Send them both back together – it'll be neater that way. Liaise with Scem, and see the trip goes without a hitch. Wait out on that though – there might be the need to send our new Mage somewhere as well – I'll let you know as soon as I can.'

'Absolutely, sir. You can count on us. Is there anything else?'

'Nothing that can't wait. I'm looking into that proposed change of terminology of yours. I just need to get a copy of your uncle's memoirs and I'll take a look. Wait out on that as well. Other than that, good work both of you – carry on.'

'Thank you, sir. We'll see you soon.'

'Okay. Boss out.'

'And ... connection's off. Well, what do you think of that?'

'He's thinking about it. I mean, having a unit of energy officially *named after me...'*

'Not that!'

'Oh, you mean the appearance of a Mage in the L-Shaped Village? Yes that's a shock alright. Especially one so powerful. I mean, they're usually pretty strong, but not on that scale...'

'No, not that either – keeping us in the dark about a lost soul!'

'Oh yes, that is quite strange. And why did the Fragment trouble itself to search out Arthur just for that? And is it going back with him or will it return? It's an enigma alright. Still, ours is not to reason why and all that – scan the logs for the return trip error.'

'Okay, bringing it up. How far back shall I go?'

'No idea. Just run a representation graph and look for the peak. We'll spot it eventually.'

'Okay ... coming up now. Hmm, nothing this last year. Or the one before that. Going back another five years. Still nothing – all seems fine. Nothing for the past decade even. Are you sure this is right?'

'Where did the order come from, Pud?'

'Fair enough. Okay, let's look long term. Bringing up the last three decades. No peaks at all. Bringing up the three before that – ahh! There it is. Two went, three returned. Just there, see?'

'Oh yes. That's unusual. That's what happens when you put tech into the hands of amateurs, Pud – they miss things. We wouldn't have missed that in a million years. Okay, start the prep for an unauthorised trip correction – one jump, two destinations – that'll use a lot of power. Let me know when you have the exact coordinates – I'll make us a Stroth-Brew.'

'YOU'RE making the Stroth-Brews now? Are you feeling okay?'

'Dough drops, Pud?'

'Erm, yes please. Err – Thanks.'

Chapter Fifteen

Danny's Tale

As they neared the village, Art could make out the villagers lining the street outside the row of houses making up the L-shape. They were all cheering and greeting the victorious soldiers as they returned, still marching in formation. When the soldiers were a few feet away, Sergeant barked a command from the front and they all dispersed, running into the arms of their loved ones, some of whom were smiling, some crying, but all looking proud of their army as they disappeared into the crowd.

Art was last in, with Shay-la, Maga, Hité, Scem, Zurioa and of course Danny, the formidable leader of the Blue Triangle army, now just a lost little boy trying to get home. The soldiers had all heard the exchange during the battle, but the villagers had been too far away. As the little contingent came within clear view there were smiles and cheers, but one by one they caught sight of Danny, still YerDichh to them, and they all looked shocked. Art couldn't tell if it was anger or something else, but slowly, complete silence descended over the whole village as their enemy walked arm in arm with Scem's second-in-command, the Keeper of the Horn, the guardian of the Scriptures. They stopped in front of the Horn Keeper Inn, the entrance still blocked by speechless villagers who made no move to let them through.

Jonnoe was the first to speak. He pushed his way through the crowd and fronted up to them. He looked at Shay-la, utterly incredulous that she was allowing it, and then turned to Scem.

'*What* is the meaning of this?' he demanded.

Art had never heard anyone be so bold as to speak to Scem in this way. Scem's face took on an expression of anger, but he controlled it and spoke calmly.

'You will see. Let us by; that is *not* a request.'

Jonnoe did not move at first, but he looked at his wife and something in her eyes reassured him. He stepped aside. Scem walked forward into the clearing and spoke loudly, with the leader's voice Art had heard him use before.

'By now you are all probably wondering why our enemy is in our midst. You are all probably outraged that he is here at all, and I wouldn't blame you. But this is *not* the time for judgment. He has a story to tell, and I urge you to listen. Many of you will feel like you have scores to settle, old wounds still unhealed. But be reminded, that is not our way. And I will not tolerate any instances of such. Let me tell you, after he has spoken you will not feel the need. We will sit, warm ourselves, drink and listen. And then we will help.' He turned to Danny, smiled and beckoned him to follow.

Hité walked with him up the steps of the Horn Keeper and into the warmth of the huge room. Art followed with Shay-la and Maga, and finally Jonnoe, still looking sceptical, who joined his wife as she passed.

Scem sat Danny down in one of the huge chairs by the fire and the little contingent sat around him as the other villagers filed in, muttering under their breath. Hité was reassuring Danny.

'I'm okay,' he said. 'I will explain myself. I must do this.'

Art had almost forgotten that this little boy's mind was nearly fifty years old. It was very difficult to comprehend.

After a while Sergeant joined them, placing a huge tray of steaming tankards down on the low table between the chairs surrounding the fire. They all took one, except Danny, who had his handed to him by Shay-la. Jonnoe looked at her disapprovingly. They all took a sip and instantly the aroma overwhelmed Art's senses with feelings of calm and rest. Just the smell was enough, but the warmth of it moving down his throat into his chest was the most amazing feeling after the day he'd had. There was also a large plate of what looked like little balls of dough on the table, with a small container of clear honey at the side.

181

'Try one of these, Art. They're dough drops,' Hité said. She took one for herself, dipped it into the honey and ate it.

Art tried one. They were quite simply the tastiest thing he had ever had. They were still warm, and they complemented the Stroth-Brew perfectly.

'Danny?' Hité said, provoking quizzical looks from some of the villagers.

'I'll pass if it's all the same.'

He looked quite pale, and Art couldn't help but feel sorry for him again. He had been stripped of his youth, of an upbringing with his family, and Art couldn't begin to imagine what that must have been like.

'Okay then,' she said, 'are you ready for this?'

Danny looked at her and nodded faintly.

Scem stood up and spoke. 'I was a young man of twenty-four and had not yet arrived here, but I'm sure most of you can remember when YerDichh first arrived in this village. To all of you he probably seemed like a young man in his twenties. But he has a shocking truth to tell you, the likes of which neither you nor I have ever heard. I urge you to listen; do not judge.' He turned to Danny. 'When you are ready,' he said, and sat back down.

Danny looked afraid. 'Must I stand up for this?' he asked Hité.

'No,' she said.

'It's just, well I don't know where to start.'

'Just go with what you can remember.'

Danny nodded and took a deep breath. He closed his eyes, as if searching for the memory. Eventually, he found it.

'It was dark, the middle of the night I think. I heard something downstairs that woke me with a start, so I went to investigate. I wanted to see what he'd left behind. I crept down the stairs and heard footsteps coming from the living room, so I crept up to the doorway and peeked into the room. There was … a strange little man with a … a *bottle*, it looked like. He was taking the sherry and some other things, and it scared me. I didn't know what to do, but I was so scared that I just ran at him screaming. Then there

182

was a flash of light and a feeling of falling through leaves and branches, and I landed on the ground in a forest. I didn't know where I was, but I was scared and couldn't stop crying. I crawled for hours, trying to go … *anywhere* really. I didn't know what I was doing. But then the trees disappeared and I can remember seeing blue sky and two huge mountains, and a cart full of people. They stopped and helped me up onto the back and kept asking me questions about where I was going, but I couldn't tell them. The next thing I remember was being freezing cold and I was crying again, and being told to jump down from the cart and walking into someone's house. They fed me and gave me some clothes, and I slept in one of their chairs. I was so confused; I just wanted to go back home. No one would tell me anything. They just kept saying I should get back to work, but it didn't make any sense to me. I walked the street for ages, trying to work out where I was. No one would help, they just asked me why I wasn't doing anything.' He stopped.

Hité put a hand on his. 'And how old were you, Danny?'

'I was barely seven. I had had my birthday party the day before.'

Scem looked round at the villagers. 'A seven-year-old *human* child, walking our streets,' he said.

There were gasps from everyone.

'A human who stole from my shop!' one of the villagers called out.

Danny reacted swiftly. 'I was *seven*! I was hungry! What was I supposed to do? What would one of *your* children do if you didn't feed him?' he pleaded.

The villager fell silent.

'Go on,' Hité encouraged.

'I couldn't understand why no one would help me. The family who had taken me in started to get angry with me and I didn't know why. I was only a child and I just got angry back; I didn't know any better. So I started taking things from them as well, food, clothes – it had always been alright at home so I just thought that's what I should do. But then I wasn't allowed back into

183

their house, so I had to take things from wherever I could find them. I grew up on the streets, freezing cold and always hungry. I can't remember how long things stayed like that, but I know it was years. Too long for a small child to be out in the cold. After a while I got good at telling stories about who I was, and even better at taking things. But it wasn't long before I was caught. I was brought into a big house and asked all sorts of questions: who was I, where had I come from, where was I going? Questions I couldn't really answer; it had all just blurred into nothingness. The name YerDichh just came to me; it was a name my big brother used to call me. He used to save his pocket money each week and buy a big bar of chocolate, and I used to ask him for some and he'd say, "Get lost, YerDichh." I don't know what it meant, but I liked my brother. So I was YerDichh from then on.'

Art had the irresistible urge to laugh out loud, but managed to stifle it. Hité noticed.

'Art?' she said.

'Erm, it's just … I don't think he was calling you *YerDichh*, Danny.'

'Oh?' he replied. 'What then?'

'I think it was more like "Get lost ..." erm, you know what – never mind.'

Danny continued. 'After that I started working every now and then, doing little jobs around the village and getting to know everyone. But I was still angry inside, really angry. And really that's all I can remember about my time here in the village. *Anger*. Anger about not being able to go home, about missing my family, about being told I should be working when a child should be *playing* and being *looked after*. I was just left to fend for myself and I resented *everyone* for it. And it wasn't long before that anger turned to *hate*. Big, red, all-consuming *hate*. I don't know how many years I'd been in the village, but it was a long time. Possibly longer than I'd been at home, and eventually accepted I was never going back. So I left. I just picked a direction and walked. I headed back towards the two big hills I remembered seeing and kept walking. And then I met Dabellar. He was walking with a

184

stout little man who seemed to know what I was thinking, and they started asking me all kinds of questions about the village and what it was hiding. I didn't know what they were talking about, but even when I didn't answer them they seemed happy with me. So I went with them. And for the first time since I could remember, I *fitted in*. These people liked me, liked it when I talked of hating the village and all of its people. And for some reason their soldiers feared me and I could make them do anything I wanted, and before I knew what was happening they'd made me their leader – I have *no idea* how that happened. But I was useful and felt needed. And then, from nowhere, I started having urges to come back here, with my army, and conquer this place. My feelings of hate were resurfacing, but far worse than I could remember. It became an obsession, something I couldn't stop thinking about…' He paused.

Hité leaned closer. 'Did you ever find out who the stout little man was, Danny?'

He took a while to answer. 'Why do you ask?'

'Because I have a feeling that those weren't *entirely* your own thoughts,' she said.

There were more little gasps from the villagers. Even Scem looked taken aback; I don't think even he had thought of that.

'But that's not *possible* … is it?' he said, a little louder than he intended.

'A clever Mage, working with an accomplished Mind-Charm – it's possible, yes,' she replied. 'After all – we all heard how he was controlling you – its possible he was actually changing your thoughts at the same time.'

'My word,' Scem said under his breath.

Danny looked angry now. Very angry. 'All those times, all those attacks, I was … *made* to think that was the right thing to do?'

'I'm sorry, but it isn't quite that simple,' Hité said. 'The anger you felt *was* your own, but probably amplified many times over. They used you, Danny. They sensed you knew the village well and that you resented us for

185

letting you grow up in that appalling way, and they used it to try to get what they wanted.'

The villagers all looked very shocked. The crowd parted and a stout little man with a bright white beard emerged, wearing a leather apron and highly polished boots. He looked apologetically at Danny.

'I ... I never knew,' he said, 'none of us did. You looked so *old*; if we'd known you were just a human child, we'd ... well I don't know what we'd have ... I'm so sorry...'

Danny looked up at him and narrowed his eyes. 'You're ... the shopkeeper.'

'I am Wan-Seg, yes.'

'You threw me out into the snow. I was hungry, just hungry.' He said this with no anger, just a blank expression.

'Yes, I know and I am sorry. Truly sorry, Yer ... er ... Danny.' Wan-Seg slowly held out his hand for Danny to shake.

Danny stood up, his face unreadable; Hité kept hold of his hand. Danny and the shopkeeper stood facing each other for what seemed like an eternity, the silence almost deafening. Then slowly Danny brought his hand up and shook Wan-Seg's, a solitary tear rolling down his cheek. The Horn Keeper Inn erupted in a great cheer, and Wan-Seg embraced Danny with a sombre look on his face.

'I am so sorry, Danny,' he said over the noise.

'But ... the things I did ... *I* should be apologising.'

'It's forgotten. Forgotten, do you hear me?'

Danny looked mortified. 'I'm not sure I deserve this,' he said, and broke free from Wan-Seg's grip.

Hité smiled warmly and took his hand again. 'You have paid the price many times over already; your childhood, your family. This is nothing compared to that.'

Danny's face was drained of emotion.

186

'BUT...' Hité said, with a glint in her eyes, 'I told you there were people who could help you.'

Danny's face lit up momentarily. 'They can get me home?' he said.

'Yes.'

'But won't they ... my family, I mean ... won't they all be ... *old*?'

Hité smiled even wider. 'Absolutely not.'

A spark of hope lit up Danny's face, but he looked confused. 'What do you mean?'

'Did they tell you anything about Portals, Danny?'

'Not really. I was more concerned with just finding it, winning it, controlling it.' He paused. 'I guess they must have suppressed any other desires I had.'

'Have you looked at yourself in the mirror lately?' Hité asked.

'What should I expect to see?'

'Just yourself, as you were when you first arrived here. Sure, your face has the inevitable odd line of "experience", a consequence of so much Time in another world. But you haven't aged.'

'Your point being?'

'Humans in our world aren't affected by Time, and vice versa. So a Portal can't take you *through* Time, even an artificial one, unless they're specifically shifted in a certain direction. Don't you see?'

Danny's eyes glazed over in thought.

Art was lost again. 'What does that mean, Hité?' he asked.

'Let Danny work it out – he deserves that at least.'

And slowly Danny's eyes lit up and fixed on Hité. 'I'll be ... I'll be right back from where I was taken ... and ... *when* ... I was taken!'

'That's right. A Portal can take you back to where you were taken from and, if you desire, to exactly *when* as well.'

'I'll be a child again – it'll be like I never left!' Danny saw the look in Hité's eyes and his face fell.

'I'm afraid it's not that simple,' she said, looking truly sorry for him.

187

'Why? Why isn't it that simple?'

'Your mind has grown, Danny. You've been here *forty* years. That can't be undone; I'm afraid you won't *feel* like a child at all.'

Danny looked like the world had been pulled from under him, just as it was starting to right itself.

'So what will happen when I go back?'

Hité sighed, choosing her words carefully. 'You won't remember, not at first. It will be like it never happened. But in time, you *will* remember. Your mind will not let go of those memories, however much you want it to. They're a part of you now. That can't change; I'm sorry.'

Shay-la looked more annoyed than any of them. 'You see – this is what happens when you mess with things that should be left alone. This poor boy has lost everything, and it's all because of two immature men sat in front of a computer screen. It's outrageous!'

'No, no, hang on a minute,' Art said. 'This isn't all bad, Danny.'

'How do you mean? How can it get any *better*?' he replied.

'Listen; it's happened – you can't change that, no one can. But just think – how many times have all of us thought "if I had my time over again, I'd do things differently"? It's because we were so young at the time and we didn't know any better.'

There was silence.

'Seriously,' he continued, 'how many times have we *all* thought that at some point? Be honest with yourselves. I should have tried harder at school, I shouldn't have tried to do that without help, those sorts of things.'

The odd murmur of agreement came from the crowd.

'Go on,' Scem said, looking intrigued.

'Well Danny *has* that chance. He can go through his childhood again, but with an *adult* mind. He can look around at his peers and see the mistakes they make *because* they're so young, the wrong decisions they take because they don't know any better. The wisdom of old age, the vitality of youth. He can think things through first, the way a child can't. You've been given a great gift, Danny … if you choose to see it that way.'

Danny narrowed his eyes, unsure of what Art was saying.

'My word,' Scem said, 'he's right. All those years of wisdom, and he's just starting out. They say we learn by our mistakes – and Danny's made *plenty* of those – no offence, Danny.'

Danny was still looking confused. 'Erm, none taken. I think.'

'Listen, Danny,' Art went on, 'I may be wrong, but I'm sensing you're feeling a great deal of regret about the things you've done as YerDichh, am I right?'

Danny nodded.

'Well then! You've been taught the greatest lesson of right and wrong anyone will ever learn. And from now on you can choose the path you will walk through life, with an exceptional moral compass. *Use* it, Danny, to do things *your* way. What do you say?'

Danny sat for a while in total silence, thinking hard, everyone around him hopeful that something good could come out of this tragedy. A middle-aged man in the body of a seven-year-old child starting all over again. Would he be able to cope with it all? School, parents, brothers and sisters – all the things usually seen through the eyes of a child, and oblivious to how hard, or sometimes how easy, it can be because of it? And would he be able to go back to a world where he *wasn't* in charge, where he would have to follow *orders*, be subservient? Art tried to think how he would feel if it were him, but after only a few moments his mind boggled and he had to slap himself. He just hoped that Danny's experiences as an adult in *this* world had made him strong enough to cope with the prospect of growing up again in another.

After what seemed like an eternity Danny smiled, and his eyes twinkled with wonder. 'You're right,' he said, 'it'll be hard at first, going to ... urgh ... *school*, but I'll be seeing things so much more clearly because of my experiences here.' He stood up. 'It'll be amazing. When do I go?'

189

And another cheer erupted around him, with much shoulder-patting and back-slapping. He looked so happy at everyone's reactions that Art thought he wouldn't want to leave.

Hité walked up to Art. 'And you say you're nothing special,' she said, a wry smile on her face. 'Don't you believe it.'

Eventually, the furore died down when one of Scem's soldiers came in from the snow and handed him a note.

'Excuse me, sir – top-priority communication from the Helm.'

Scem took the note. 'Thank you, Raker. Stay and have a Stroth-Brew, won't you?' 'Oh thank you, sir, I think I will!'

'Good man. Now – what's this all about?' Scem scanned the page, then handed it to Hité.

'Ah, I wondered when we'd get to you, Art,' Hité said, and gave a melancholy smile.

'What does it say?' Art said eagerly.

Hité handed it to Sergeant, but didn't keep Art waiting.

'It's a communication from Pud and Jimma. It contains details of your return, Arthur.' She looked at Danny. 'And yours.' She looked at Maga. 'And ... *yours*.'

Maga stared at her wide-eyed and Shay-la gave a gasp as her tankard fell crashing to the floor.

Chapter Sixteen
The Golden Three

Shay-la stood up, looking panic-stricken.

'What do you mean by that exactly?' she demanded.

Hité stood up as well and tried to calm her down.

'Shay-la, your son is a *Mage*. You must have expected this.'

'Yes, but ... going *there*? Through one of those mad-men's electric Portals?'

Scem could see that Maga was looking apprehensive to say the least, and slightly angry that he was being spoken *about* so much. Scem spoke to him directly to try to put him at ease.

'Maga, Pud and Jimma have received a communication from your Instructors.'

'Wh ... what, *already*?' Maga stammered.

Scem nodded reassuringly. 'Yes, Maga. It seems that for the first part of your training they want you to experience life as a human, in the human world.'

'F ... for how long?' Maga asked.

Shay-la looked outraged. 'But that's not how the training works – it's never been done like that before! WHAT ARE THEY THINKING?' she screamed.

'Shay-la, please try to calm down,' Hité said, taking Shay-la's hands in her tentative way. 'Maga will be returned to exactly when he left; he'll be gone literally no time at all.'

Shay-la broke hands with Hité angrily. 'I'm not thinking of *me* – how long will it be for Maga?'

191

'The note doesn't say exactly,' said Jonnoe, who now had the paper in his hand. 'Shay-la, we must encourage him on this. The Instructor's words are final, and it could be good for Maga. This is a *good* thing, my love.'

Shay-la looked at Jonnoe, her eyes still wide in panic. 'But ... *my boy*...' She wrapped her arms around Maga and squeezed him hard.

'Honey, we have time. The Portal's not until tomorrow,' Jonnoe said.

Shay-la let Maga go reluctantly, but kept her arm linked through his.

'I'm going ... *home*?' Art said quietly.

Hité turned to him, a look of understanding in her eyes. With everyone's attention firmly on the dramatic turn of events for Danny and Maga, she had almost forgotten how strange all this still was for Art. She patted his shoulder.

'You've done what you were sent here to do, Art, so ... yes,' she said.

'But ... I haven't *done* anything,' he protested.

'No, not physically anyway. At least not yet.'

'Which means?' Art said.

'Danny has been found; I'm absolutely *sure* that was the reason you were sent here. All that was needed was your presence, nothing more. But the Scriptures *do* mention this – the Prophecy is coming true; think back – do you remember?'

Art thought back to when Hité had shown him the Scriptures on the Sacred Horn and he *could* remember something about a first coming.

Scem closed his eyes in recollection: *On the ten-thousandth moonset, before the First Great Battle, look towards the Sun and Snow Hut, and walking through the snow shall be the Great Unitor, and He shall show you the way. Listen to him with understanding on the first coming, and on the second coming, when he shall stay forever, he shall know his calling. Draw upon his knowledge then, and then alone.* Scem opened his eyes and took Hité's hands. 'I see it now. I'm sorry for doubting the Scriptures, my love. It will never happen again.'

Hité looked into Scem's eyes, her own glistening slightly. 'It all fits,' she said, 'the trick is to *let* it fit.'

'Ahem. Er ... excuse me...' Art said, 'I still don't get it. And in any case, what about *this*?' He held up his wrist. Still securely fastened by the long leather twine was the Fragment.

The villagers, including Sergeant, drew breath collectively at the sight.

But Scem and Hité looked as calm as ever. 'You're important, Art,' Hité said, 'and the Fragment knows that; it would have sought you out sooner or later with or without this. The first part of the Prophecy of the Scriptures has happened, and it happened *with* the Fragment in tow. The question is, did it *come* here with you, or did it *bring* you?'

Art thought for a second. 'Why is that important?'

Scem grinned knowingly. 'It's important because it could mean you are someone *very* important indeed.'

'I have *no* doubt of that,' said Jonnoe, beaming at Art.

'Oh?' said Hité.

'You haven't heard, have you?'

'Heard what?' said Scem.

'I have discovered Art's skill.'

Everyone looked at him expectantly – Scem wasn't the only one who could command impressive silences.

'Well?' said Scem impatiently.

Jonnoe reached into his tunic and pulled out a very new-looking hat. It was almost an exact replica of his own, a few sizes smaller but with the same emblem embossed with dark resin on the side. He looked at Maga.

'I hope this is alright with you, son,' he said, 'it was really meant for you ... I was so sure ... but you know I'm proud of you, don't you?'

Maga smiled as much as his anxiety allowed. 'Of course I know, Dad. It's okay, really.'

Jonnoe smiled broadly, walked over to Art and placed it firmly on his head. He stood back and folded his arms, looking impressed.

193

'*Now* he has a hat,' he said.

Hité smiled, but Scem looked a little disappointed. Maga looked at Art and tilted his head as if trying to work something out. And then it was his turn to gasp.

'So if the Fragment *did* bring him here, and he's a ... then he could be ... you're not serious?'

Scem wagged his finger at Maga. 'Ah ah, now then – you know the rules.'

Maga looked at Art with amazing respect in his eyes, but he shook it off and looked away again.

'No, no, that can't be. Get a grip, Maga,' he said to himself.

Art nearly let out a sarcastic 'hurumph' that *Maga* was finding something hard to believe – Art's head was still spinning about how he already knew this boy, but far into his future.

Jonnoe held the paper Scem had given him closer to his eyes. 'In any case, I think the three of you had better get acquainted.'

'Why's that?' Shay-la enquired.

'Because by the looks of things you're not only going through together, you're all headed for the same place.'

'Are ... are you *sure*?' Shay-la asked.

Scem held his hand out and Jonnoe passed him the sheet. Scem studied it closely.

'Not only that, but the same *Time*, give or take a month or two,' Jonnoe continued.

Art and Danny looked at each other.

'Are you sure that's right?' Art said.

Scem nodded. 'It seems so. Why do you ask?'

'We're from the *same* Time? Is that even possible? I mean, Danny's been *here* for four decades.'

194

'Oh it's possible alright,' said Jonnoe. 'An accidental fall into a Portal can take you anywhere. He was lucky it was only forty years – could have been a lot worse.'

Art mulled this over for a while. 'So we're from the same place, and the same Time. How can that be a coincidence?'

'It may not be,' said Scem. 'We've already seen the strange ways the events described in the Scriptures are manifesting. If I were you, I wouldn't try to understand them. As Hité said, these things all fit – the trick is to *let* them.'

Hité slipped an arm around Scem's waist and squeezed him proudly.

'I think he's right,' said Danny. 'The things I've seen since I've been here, the strange things that have happened; thinking about it too much won't *do* anything to help. If I were you, I'd let it be. After all, I'm going home ... and so are you. Hey, I might even see you there.' He smiled.

It was the first time Art had seen him smile properly, and it made Art smile too.

'You're right, you're absolutely right – we *are* going home.' Art handed Danny and Maga their tankards and then picked up his own. 'Here's to it then. Here's to *home*.'

He and Danny bumped their tankards and took a slurp. Reluctantly, Maga did the same. Art smiled and patted his shoulder.

'So, for Danny and myself it's all about to end; but for you it's just beginning. But whatever the reason, the three of us are leaving here tomorrow, together. The ... the Golden Three.'

Hité and Scem looked at each other, open-mouthed.

'What?' said Art.

'Oh, nothing. It's nothing,' Scem said quickly. He raised his tankard too. 'To the Golden Three!'

The whole room raised their tankards to the same toast, then drained them all at once. Shay-la was just as enthusiastic, but her face was still tinged with sadness.

'So when do we leave?' Art asked.

'Sun-up tomorrow. Do you think you could lead us back to the spot where you arrived, Art?' said Scem.

'Erm, I think so, yes. Why's that?'

'The more constants there are regarding a Portal, the easier the calculations will be for Pud and Jimma. It'll make the whole trip much safer.'

Shay-la scoffed and held Maga's arm even tighter.

'Don't worry, Art,' Scem said, seeing the concern on his face, 'it's perfectly safe. You got here okay, didn't you?'

'We don't know exactly *how* he got here yet,' Shay-la cut in, 'but I bet it was a lot safer than anything conjured up by those two clowns!'

'Just ignore her,' Sergeant laughed. 'She's a tech-phobe. Don't worry – you'll be fine.'

Art wasn't worried. The only thing on his mind was getting home and he didn't care how he got there. He even felt happy that he wasn't going alone for some reason. He also had a funny feeling that it wasn't the end of something, but like something was *starting*. And just as Maga had no idea what he was going to experience, Art couldn't shake the feeling that something was waiting for him on the other side of that Portal too. Not just getting back to his life – although the prospect of seeing Evi again was doing a pretty good job of dominating his thoughts – but something more; something that he had already worked out but couldn't remember the answer to. Then there was the question he still hadn't worked out yet; *where was he*? But now that he was going home that question felt less important, and in any case he was tired, both physically and mentally, and he slumped back down into his chair to enjoy the atmosphere around him.

Everyone was talking excitedly; Shay-la and Jonnoe were fussing over Maga, Scem and Hité were whispering enthusiastically, Sergeant was chatting to Danny, and every now and then Art caught bits of conversation while the fire heated them all to the core. But after a few hours his eyelids

196

grew heavy and he noticed himself missing bits of what was being said until he fell asleep right there in the huge soft chair, dreaming of his own room, his own things, his family and, of course, Evi.

*

Art woke with a start, still sat in his chair, to the sound of absolute silence, the kind when it snowed back home and everything was still because of the disruption. The Horn Keeper was empty and the fire had burnt itself down to a few glowing embers that were still pumping out an impressive amount of heat. It was morning already – he had slept the whole evening and through the night – and bright light was pushing its way through the snow-covered windowpanes. In the chair to his left Danny was still fast asleep, but almost as if in answer to Art's stirring, his eyes opened and he looked around, taking in his surroundings.

'Morning,' Art said; 'looks like we slept in.'

Danny stretched and yawned. 'Hmm, I haven't done that in a while,' he said eventually.

They sat in silence for a while, taking their time to wake up in their comfortable surroundings.

'So we're going home today then. How do you feel about that, Danny?' Art said, after stretching and yawning himself.

Danny raised his eyebrows. 'I honestly don't know, to tell you the truth. My life here has been so ... real, and for so long. I'm supposed to be going *back*, but ... it feels like I'm going somewhere *new*. But I've learnt a lot since I've been here – enough to know that someone *is* meddling in your affairs.'

Art's ears pricked up. 'Oh? How do you know that?'

'I knew the moment Hité mentioned the word *Prophecy*. Dead giveaway.'

'I don't know much about any of that stuff. Why is that a dead giveaway?'

'Because there are no such things as Prophecies,' Danny said.

Art thought this was quite a statement. 'But how do you explain the things that have happened already described in the Scriptures? You're not going to tell me you think it's just coincidence, are you?'

'No, it's even simpler than that. What people think of as Prophecies are just descriptions of events that have somehow found their way back into the *past*. If those descriptions are found, in a readable form, by someone connected to those events, it's easy to think of them as a foretelling of some sort. You can see how desirable it would be for an individual if they were thought of as prophetic.'

'Yeah, I suppose so,' Art agreed.

'And most of the time,' Danny continued, 'it doesn't happen by accident.'

'You mean it can be *intentional*?'

'It usually is.' Danny leaned closer. 'Okay, imagine there's something in your past you want changed. How do you do it?'

Art thought for a moment. 'Well, presuming you can go back to before it happened, you ... stop it from happening somehow.'

'Exactly, you go back. But there are dangers to that. For example, being stuck there, being discovered, changing something by accident you didn't want to change, any number of things. But what if there was a much less risky option? Wouldn't you want to explore it?'

'Well, yes,' Art said, 'but like what?'

'It's obvious, isn't it? You send back a snippet of information. A ... *pointer*, if you like. And you leave it somewhere it's likely to be found.'

'But what would that do? I mean ... oh.'

'You're getting it now. If someone knows their own future, or even shares their knowledge of someone *else's* future, it becomes unstable. Maybe there's enough in the snippet to know if it was the right choice or not – they might decide differently when the time comes. Or, if it was an accident that someone then knows how to avoid. Sure, it's a much less

198

reliable option than actually going back and changing something directly – it might all happen the way it was going to anyway, but it's a million times safer. You send back a pointer about the future and it becomes ... you guessed it, a *Prophecy*.'

Art gasped. He took a deep breath, trying to clear his head and digest it all. 'Whoa! So what does this mean?' he said.

'That's impossible to tell. To me, the fact that there is a so-called Prophecy is proof that someone *is* trying to change something. But there's really only one thing you have to work out.'

'And what's that?'

Danny looked him square in the eyes. 'Is someone trying to *make* you, or *destroy* you?'

Art was chilled to the core.

Just then the front door burst open and Scem and Hité waltzed in.

'Good morning!' they both chimed.

In behind them came Shay-la and Maga, with Jonnoe and Fallow in tow, and finally Sergeant. Shay-la was still holding onto Maga's arm for dear life, and she looked pale and frightened. They were all clutching a steaming mug of Stroth-Brew, except Sergeant and Hité who were carrying *two* mugs each.

'We've had a communication from Pud and Jimma – the Portal will open in half an hour,' said Scem. 'That should give us plenty of time.'

Sergeant and Hité handed over their extra mugs. 'We couldn't let you leave without one last Stroth-Brew though,' said Sergeant. 'Drink up, and we'll get you out of here.'

Art noticed Shay-la tighten her grip on Maga's arm. He saw his new hat draped over the arm of the chair, picked it up and placed it on his head. Hité smiled her warmest smile. Then they all drained their mugs as quickly as they could and silently headed out into the snow.

The street was lined with people, who all cheered when they emerged. At first, Art thought they were seeing him off in the same way he had arrived, but then he noticed a few of them holding up hastily painted signs wishing

199

their Mage a safe journey. They were *all* there for Maga; none of them even looked at Art, or Danny. Having a Mage in the village was obviously a bigger deal than Art had realised. Shay-la beamed as she accompanied her son across the road to the cheers and shouts of the well-wishers, and though it made her cry, her smile was as wide as ever. Art had to fight a tear back himself at the sight of Shay-la's strength, only now starting to appreciate its many forms.

Slowly, the sound of the crowd died away as they walked further and further away from the village, and soon it was lost in the blur of falling snow. As they crunched along in silence, Art couldn't help but feel sadness in the pit of his stomach as he realised he was going to miss the L-Shaped Village: the lights coming into view before anything else, the little lamp-lit high street, the cosiness of the Horn Keeper Inn, the unbelievable comfort of both the beds he had slept in and the incredible ice rink he never got the chance to try. But he knew he would miss the people the most. Hité had shown him kindness and understanding, the likes of which he had never experienced before; Scem had shown him the value of true leadership, even though he knew he would never be able to emulate it; Sergeant had shown him how an unbelievable strength of character can save everyone when all hope is seemingly lost. But Shay-la and her family would leave the biggest hole in his heart. She had been fearless in the face of the enemy, unbelievably skilled in overcoming them, and at the same time the beautiful centrepiece of a warm family home, respected and loved, a tower of strength in all its forms. Jonnoe had trusted her opinion of Art when no one else would, taken him into the precious sanctum of his woodwork shop and helped him understand so many things that were confusing him. Fallow had made him laugh harder than he had for a long time with his unintentional wit, his resolve of iron and his mother's fearlessness. And then there was Maga. His old friend he knew very well, with whom he had plotted, schemed and laughed, but who barely knew him in this world. He wasn't sure which version of Maga he liked best; older Maga, who was brilliant and

200

trustworthy, always with an answer or a trick, or younger Maga, who was innocent, shy and still finding his feet. Art wanted to see how he would develop into the powerful Mage he knew already. And then he remembered Maga was coming with him – he *would* see it, and the feeling of something starting, not ending, grew stronger inside him.

All of the things that made him sad didn't lessen his feeling of elation at the prospect of going home though. He had missed everything and everyone so much, and the thought of it made him feel desperately sorry for Danny, who had endured decades of what Art was feeling, and at such a young age. He couldn't imagine how Danny was feeling, and he looked over at him. Danny's face was unreadable. Art walked over and nudged him as they approached the Sun and Snow Hut. Danny gave him a very adult smile as they filed in through the door to take off their winter coats.

Scem clasped his hands together. 'Well, this is it then. Can you remember the exact spot, Art?'

'It's through the woods over there – maybe four or five hundred yards or so.'

'Oh, we'd better hurry then. Is everyone ready?'

Shay-la sniffed loudly and Jonnoe held her hand. Maga was looking surprisingly calm; he didn't have his mother's strength, but he had been blessed with his father's resolve.

'Mother,' he said, 'I'll be home before you know it.'

'I know that, it's just ... you'll be ... *different* ... grown up. And I'm going to miss it.'

'I know. But you mustn't worry, I'm in good hands.' He looked at Art, then Danny. Both gave him a nod. 'I think we're ready, Scem,' said Maga, finality in his voice.

'Okay then, let's do this,' Scem said reassuringly.

They all filed out of the Sun and Snow Hut and headed towards the gap in the trees. It was much warmer there, the sun pressing through the canopy of trees and creating pools of sunlight on the ground as they entered the woods. Art walked with Danny all the way, making sure he was okay, while Shay-la was doing her best to slow everyone down. She had a longing in her eyes that told of her reluctance to let go of the son she knew and accept back one she didn't. Maga noticed it too.

'Mum, I'll still be me when I get back. I won't have changed.'

'Oh yes you will – I know it. But it's ... it's good, this is a good thing. Yes, your father's right.' She sounded like she was trying to convince herself more than anyone else. She looked over at Art. 'You will look after him, won't you? Help him, and take care of him,' she pleaded.

Art hadn't thought about that yet. He was so blinded by the thought of going back it simply hadn't occurred to him that he might unintentionally have a part to play in Maga's 'training', whatever that entailed. But the thought of *not* making sure he was okay on the other side hadn't occurred to him either.

'Don't worry about a thing. Me and Maga – we're like *that*,' he said, and linked his two index fingers together.

It was true, they were; just not *this* version of Maga. Art unlinked his fingers, and reached for his Sta'an. He handed it to her, and she resheathed it next to her own. Shay-la let go of Maga's arm briefly and hugged Art again, whispering a thank you in his ear. Then she linked her arm with Maga's again, reluctantly picking up the pace at Scem's request.

Art noticed a familiar pattern in the canopy above and looked down at the ground for the spot at which he had arrived. It wasn't difficult to recognise; there was a small circular clearing, covered with decaying leaves and little pools of sunlight.

'This is it,' he said.

They all gathered round. Art looked down at the Fragment on his wrist. He wasn't quite sure what was going to happen, but he knew in his heart that the Fragment would take him back. The ache in his chest to be back with his family gave him a little sharp pang as a reminder. Scem and Hité had said it was a planned trip, but *would* it happen on its own? He wasn't sure.

202

'Okay, it should be anytime now,' Scem said quietly.

It was too much for Shay-la to bear, and tears started streaming down her face. She flung her arms around her son, who was starting to look apprehensive himself. Eventually, she released him, and Maga stood proud and shook hands with his father. Jonnoe pulled him into a crushing hug as well, and Art could see a solitary tear rolling down his cheek.

'I'm proud of you, son,' he said. 'This is your destiny right here, and even though I can see you're not happy about it, you're embracing it. You've got your mother's strength. Use that, okay?'

Maga knew that wasn't true, but said, 'I ... I will.' Then he looked down at Fallow. 'And you take care of them both, okay?'

'I will, I'm a soldier.' He waved his Sta'an menacingly.

Maga chuckled. 'Make sure you do.' And with that, he stepped back into the clearing.

Danny joined him, giving him a look of reassurance.

'Good luck to you, Danny,' Hité said, 'and do yourself a favour.'

'What's that?' he asked.

'When your memory returns, look around you and remember who you *are*, not who people thought you were. Nobody blames you for what happened, and you'll need to remind yourself of that every day. But *use* your experience. Few people have so much of it so young. Now go and be the person you *want* to be.'

He grinned. 'I will, and thank you for everything.'

Epilogue

Hité turned to Art. 'As for you,' she said, 'I really thought you'd have got it by now.'

'Got what?'

'So many questions when you got here, and now you don't have any?' she said mockingly.

The only blatantly unresolved question suddenly came galloping into Art's head, but even now it seemed unimportant.

'I'm good, thanks,' he said.

She glanced over at Maga, then back to Art. 'Well, at least let us know how the next drop goes, okay?'

Art had totally forgotten Hité's mention of his 'friend in the black car', and suddenly he felt cheated out of some answers.

'How do you ... you never explained...'

'Just let us know, okay?' she said, grinning.

Art paused. 'And how do I do that exactly?'

'How do you do *what*?' Scem said, a similar grin on his face.

'Let you know – how do I ... get in touch with you all?'

Hité let out an exaggerated sigh of relief. '*FINALLY*,' she said.

Jonnoe cleared his throat. 'Are you sure you want to hear this, Art? It may just be the last piece of the puzzle.'

Art felt a strong rumble beneath his feet, and Danny's and Maga's outlines started shimmering. Sergeant gently nudged him into the centre of the clearing.

'Yes!' Art said desperately. 'How do I contact you?'

'It's simple,' said Hité. 'You just write a note, addressed to any one of us.'

Art stared at her in confusion. 'A *note*? What, on paper?'

'That's right.'

'*And then what*?'

Hité, Scem and Jonnoe were all chuckling now. 'You really want to hear this?' Hité laughed.

'Yes! Tell me!'

She leaned forward as if to whisper, but spoke just as loudly. '*Throw it on the fire.*'

Art could see everyone around the clearing gradually begin to lose their outlines as the shimmering grew and grew, and his eyes grew wide in realisation of what Hité had just said.

'Goodbye, Art,' she called.

Art gasped. 'You've got to be ... *NO WAY!*'

About the Author

Lee Fomes was born and raised in Hampshire, in a small village called Medstead. He began writing stories of total fiction for pleasure at an early age, often airing them on his unfortunate brothers and sister when they would have really rather been out in the huge expanse of garden at the back of the house, as Lee often was. His inspiration for this novel was plenty of happy Christmases at Redcote, the family home, and many more at his own home with his wife Hannah, and his twins William and Molly, all to whom this book is dedicated. He is a professional musician in the Armed Forces, and lives in Cuxton, a small closely-knit community in Kent.

26480169R00125

Made in the USA
Charleston, SC
08 February 2014